DARK MATTER

BOOK TWO OF THE STARFIRE WARS

JENETTA PENNER

DARK MATTER

ISBN: 9781728882727

Printed in the U.S.A. First printing 2018

Chapter 1

ver since the day Mom died, I became certain there is one rule. Life is unpredictable.

My mind carousels as I study one of Dad's favorite kinds of apple, now resting in my palm. The pinkish red flesh coated with a thin layer of dust contrasts Mom's shiny gold band. Mom is gone forever, but what if there were the possibility that Dad was still alive?

Without looking up, I ask Javen's Uncle Wirrin, "Where did you get this?"

He glances around and motions Javen and me toward a secluded grouping of trees.

When we are out of earshot from the others, he says, "I found about twenty. The fruit began showing up by an Intersection point two days ago, just outside Irilee. One of my scouts and I found them. At first, seeing the foreign fruit was strange, but I paid them no mind. Yet when so many appeared, I started asking questions."

"What kind of questions? Who did you ask?" Javen slips his arm around my waist as if to protect me from whatever his uncle might say.

"I spoke to Vihann and inquired if he had seen anything like seemingly random objects materializing from the other side of the Intersection," Wirrin answers.

"And?" I ask, inching closer to Wirrin.

"He admitted to transporting your father from the ship before the explosion." Wirrin shifts on his feet.

Nervousness swirls in my stomach. Should I tell Wirrin I saw Vihann, Javen's father, disappear with Dad on the video feed? Instead, I ask, "Why didn't he say anything to me at the Council meeting? He knew who I was."

We continue walking through the trees. Several flowers unfurl open on the branches, flickering with cyan hues. Wirrin pinches his lips at the sight.

"Something happened," Wirrin continues. "When my brother crossed to our side, he lost Dr. Foster."

"Lost him?" Javen asks before I get the chance. "Losing Cassi's father isn't possible."

Wirrin stops walking. "Well, that's what happened. When Vihann rematerialized on the other side, Foster was gone." Wirrin looks to me with a slight frown before watching the unfurling petals once more.

"So, then, where is he?" I ask. "People also don't vanish into thin air."

"That is the question I'm asking, too," Wirrin says.

I look down at the apple still in my grasp. "But how do you know this is from him? It could just be a piece of fruit that is somehow coming across the Intersection from Arcadia."

Wirrin shrugs. "Vihann and I met your father several times when he and your mother first visited our planet. He always seemed to have one with him. He shared the fruit with me during one meeting, and then the next time I saw him, he brought me several more from his ship. I enjoyed this Earthen delicacy immensely." Wirrin looks to me again. "What are they called?"

"Apples . . . Pink Lady variety." I stare at the fruit's pinkish red skin and sigh. Just holding this apple brings back warm memories of Dad sharing his slices with me.

"I recognized the taste immediately and thought of Dr. Foster." Wirrin's words break me from my happier thoughts and bring me back to reality. "But I knew about the explosion and his death, so I was confused. Then when the fruits kept appearing, I began to think something more was going on beyond the unexplained presence of so many apples."

"Could he be hiding on your side of the Intersection?" I ask. "Maybe he ended up at a different point than Javen's father."

Javen wrinkles his nose. "I don't know how that would be possible. The Alku sense when humans are on this side. Not right away all the time, but Foster would have been here long enough for us to locate him."

I remember the first time Javen brought me here. He was so worried the others would sense and find me.

And I don't think my father would be on Arcadia and not come to me. Even if he were hiding for some reason, there's no way he would keep me in the dark while allowing me to believe he was dead. Especially after what we both went through after Mom died. He knows the pain and loss.

"Then he must be stuck somewhere." I pinch the bridge of my nose. "Could he be inside the Intersection?"

Wirrin's brows furrow in confusion. "There's *nothing* inside the Intersection. It's only a pass-through."

"But do you know for sure?"

Javen closes any space between us. "Cassi, that's not how the Intersection works. You're only getting your hopes up."

I hold the apple in the air. "These are appearing out of nowhere by an Intersection point. Does either of you have a better explanation? And Wirrin, you're the one who told me my dad needed help. What are you wanting me to do?"

"I had hoped you might know something I didn't about your father."

"Well, maybe I do. If the Intersection is more than a pass-through and my father is trapped, I need to figure out how to get him back. Can you take me to the place the apples were found?"

Wirrin crosses his arms over his body and says nothing.

"Uncle," Javen says, "if you didn't want Cassi to have the information, you wouldn't have told her. You knew my father's choice to hold back this secret was wrong."

"If this gets out among our people, I don't know what will happen," Wirrin says.

"The Starfire chose Cassi, and the energy has bonded her to me. This may be a new era for the Alku. And if the Starfire has deemed this, we won't be able to stop the motion."

Javen's words resonate through me. How much power do the crystals have to be able to control my mind, my actions? Am I even my own person anymore? I stare at Wirrin as he speaks to Javen and bows his head slightly.

"But these are not easy words to swallow, even for me," Wirrin says. "And I am open to change when many are not."

"Please?" I ask. "I only want to know what happened to my dad. I need to see if he's safe."

Wirrin bows his head. "I'll take you, but give me time to prepare."

And with that, he turns and walks toward Irilee. I start to follow, but Javen takes my upper arm and stops me. I twist toward him and he pulls me into his embrace. The warmth of his chest and the rise and fall of his breath settle my whirling soul. I inhale his scent and press into him.

"Why are you doing all this for me?" I mutter into this shirt.

Javen loosens our embrace but still clutches my waist. The expression on his face is confused and almost sad.

He whispers, "Why do you even have to ask?"

"Javen, you disobeyed your father and the Council to be here—to be with me."

"I had hoped to change my father's mind . . . to help him see reason. But Wirrin listened. He's listening even now. My father is wise, but he's not seeing logic. There must be a way for the Alku to thrive; we can't simply let my people die out. And if you are the key in this, I want to find out what that means." He pauses for a moment. "Cassi, I would do *anything* for you."

My heart skips at his words. *Anything*? I gaze into Javen's eyes as if I'm seeing into his soul, and what I see is beautiful, pure. The intensity of our connection grips onto me and interweaves my heart and mind. I know he's telling the truth. He *would* do anything for me, and my heart aches for that—for that love and safety.

Suddenly the guilt of my own selfishness bubbles to the surface. Saving the Alku should come before me.

I take a step back from his embrace. "It's not fair to put that kind of pressure on me."

A confused look overtakes Javen's face. "What pressure? What the Starfire has gifted us is beautiful."

I scoff. "What if the Starfire is manipulating our bond? Making our feelings toward each other more important to you than saving your people?"

Javen's brown irises shift and swirl with cyan. "It's not."

"People don't fall in love like this," I say. Despite my words, my heart flutters with longing for him but I stand my ground, not giving in to its desire for me to fall back into his arms.

"Sometimes my people do. There are even rarer occasions when the crystals determine when two hearts are fated to be together." A faint smile, almost shy, plays at the corners of his mouth. "The Starfire is always right."

Javen pulls me close to him again, and I don't resist. I don't want to, even though my mind is shouting something different than my heart. His body tugs at me like a magnet. I snake my arms over his shoulders and rise onto the tips of my toes.

I whisper, "I'm just scared."

"Me too." His words come out as near breath before he touches his lips to mine and his strong hands flow over my back. "But we are stronger together."

As our lips make contact the world becomes right again, and all I can think of is Javen.

△ △ △

"Why are you still out here?" Beda asks from behind. "And with *her*?"

Heat rushes up the nape of my neck and cheeks.

Javen interlaces his fingers with mine and squares himself, making his frame appear larger than it already is.

Beda tenses her jaw. "You're making the wrong choice, cousin."

My breath comes in short pants as I squeeze Javen's fingers. Javen and Beda say nothing for what seems like an eternity, and the weight of the silence bears down on my shoulders.

Javen continues to train his icy stare onto her. "Is this all you came out here to say, Beda?

"My father needs you," she finally says, relenting.

Javen squeezes my hand. "Let's go, then."

We start to walk, but Beda holds out her arm to block me. "Not you."

"Why not?" I protest, feeling bold yet terrified of her all at the same time.

"My father has ordered me to escort you to your quarters for sleep."

I open my mouth to argue but then snap it shut. Just thinking about sleeping reminds me of how little I had last night.

Javen eyes Beda for a moment and then looks to me. "Go with her," Javen says. "Crossing the Intersection takes a great amount of energy. You will need to rest before attempting it again."

I touch my neck where the Starfire had once hung before Hammond took the crystal from me. "I'm going to need a new Starfire, too."

"I'll make sure you receive a new one," he says.

Javen leans in and kisses my forehead. A shimmer of energy ripples through my body, but as soon as he pulls back, the feeling dissipates. "See you soon." He smiles at me and then turns to walk down the main road of Irilee.

"Can we go now?" Beda asks.

I nod and follow her as she struts down a smaller side road. She stays several paces ahead, and so I speed to catch up.

"I don't get it. What's with you?" I ask.

She spins toward me and I nearly slam into her, but she blocks me with her arm—again.

"There's nothing wrong with *me*. You're the one intruding on my world. Would you want us intruding on *yours*?"

Nervousness rushes through my chest, but I hold my ground and plant my feet. "Traveling to Arcadia wasn't my choice, and I didn't make the Starfire choose me. I wanted none of this, Beda. But here I am."

We stand staring at each other for what seems like a lifetime. My pulse is pounding so strongly that I'm certain Beda can hear the sound. Her eyes swirl with deep cyan in anger.

Finally, Beda sneers. She does a one-eighty and starts walking again.

With a sigh and an admittedly very immature eye roll, I follow her. Beda's unkindness makes me miss Max and Irene all the more. I hope they're safe. I need them. I need my friends and want to get back to them as soon as I can.

Beda leads me to a small dwelling. She pushes the door open and then slams it right in my face. I want to kick in the door and pretend it's her face. Instead, I shove my way inside and then pause.

The room is simple with furnishings nothing like the type I'm used to seeing, not even on the ship or in the apartment I shared on Arcadia. A rustic table made of dark wood sits to my right, circled by four chairs fashioned from the same kind of gnarly wood. To my other side is a small kitchen. My gaze darts around and eventually rests on a large stone fireplace in the corner— no stove—and instead of a refrigerator, there's . . . nothing. Unfamiliar produce, sprouting long green stems and frilly leaves, lies on the counter.

Beda flings her hand out toward the vegetables. "Hungry?"

"Yeah, actually. I haven't eaten since yesterday."

"I'll bring you something in a minute," she mutters flatly.

She then waves me on to a room at the rear of the dwelling. Inside, a single mattress lies directly on the floor. If you can call it a mattress— more like a big pillow.

"Get some sleep. You're going to need all the rest you can manage."

I turn to ask her whose home this even is, but she's already gone. Maybe to get me food, but I doubt it. I let out a loud sigh as exhaustion creeps over my body.

I shuffle to the bed and squat to touch the surface. The fabric and stuffing give under my hand, much softer and more comfortable than I had first imagined. At the end of the bed, I grab a green blanket and crawl onto the giant pillow. The surprisingly soft blanket amply covers my body, and I begin to relax. Before long, I cross over to the world of cyan dreams, leaving Beda and my troubles behind.

$$\triangle \, \triangle \, \triangle$$

My eyes flutter open to the plunk of a wooden plate of food at the end of my bed and the shuffling footsteps of Beda hurrying from my room. I push up to sit, and my body feels completely refreshed. I don't know how; there's no way I could have slept *that* long.

My stomach grumbles and I straighten, crossing my legs with the blanket still pulled over me. I grab the plate and pick up the spoon resting in some green concoction. I sniff the mixture and, to be honest, I'm not sure about the spicy smell. But I've always been willing to try new foods. *So, let's not make this meal any different, Cassi.*

I bring the spoon to my mouth and take the bite. Slightly sweet and a little sour, but overall the cooked vegetables are not bad. I shrug and take another taste, and then another and another until the plate is empty. I push from the bed, taking my plate with me, and walk out of the room.

Beda stands in the kitchen, eating the same meal I had just devoured.

"Did you make this?" I ask, gesturing to my plate as I place it on the counter.

Beda doesn't answer and continues chewing.

"Well, if you did, the food was good," I say.

She eyes me and then tosses her empty plate to the side. "Go back to bed."

"How long was I asleep?" I peer out the window and see that the morning light is still like it was when we came in.

"Maybe thirty minutes?"

"Thirty minutes? I feel as if I slept for hours."

Beda shrugs. "The Starfire is changing you. Who knows *what* you'll be when it finishes."

Chapter 2

After Beda forces me to rest for several more hours because I'm a human, I trail behind her on the street again, her wavy, dark hair blowing in the breeze. Her words about the Starfire's effect on me burrow their way through my brain. She's just trying to scare me. Still, the thought persists.

The Starfire *is* changing me—it *has* changed me already—the visions, my new abilities. But I can't chalk one restful nap up to the crystals.

"How much sleep do you need? Do the Alku need?" I ask as I catch up with her.

She lets out a low, barely audible growl in her throat and I ease away from her. If I weren't already aware of how much she hated me, I would think I had imagined the noise. But I know better.

"Using the Starfire usually allows us to sleep a few hours each night. But we can get by on less."

"So, you think the Starfire is doing the same thing to me?"

Beda arches a brow. "I've no idea what the Starfire is doing to you, *human*."

I follow as she walks through the entrance of a structure made from natural brick. Wirrin, Javen, and another Alku girl stand inside the room. They turn toward me and Beda as we enter, and the younger female tilts her head my way. The girl is maybe a year or two older than me with bronzed skin and long, straight snow-white hair with a single braid draping down the front of her shoulder.

Javen's eyes light up when he sees me, and my heart flutters. I rush past Beda to his side. I want to feel comfortable among the Alku, but Javen is the only one who truly makes me feel welcome and safe.

"You seem more rested," he whispers. "Were you able to sleep?"

I nod and make a mental note to speak with him later about the sleep issue and other differences between the Alku and Earthlings.

"Can I go now?" Beda asks Wirrin. "I do have other . . . *tasks* to attend to."

"No," Wirrin says. "You must stay."

Beda scoffs and throws her back up against the nearest wall next to a small table, crossing her arms over her chest. "My place is out defending the Starfire fields on Arcadia," she mutters under her breath.

"I have a rotation of fifty Alku soldiers who are using the power of the Starfire to defend the fields and to keep Hammond and her ships away from Primaro," Wirrin says. "I have a better use of your talents in mind, Beda."

She groans. Wirrin ignores her annoyance and turns his head toward me. He gestures to the other girl in the room. Not only is she one of the most stunning people I've ever seen—boasting large, brown eyes and full lips—but with her exposed arms and the shape of her muscular body, it's obvious she's incredibly strong, too.

"This is Yaletha," Wirrin says. "She's the scout who found the apples at the Intersection point. She'll take you to the location."

Yaletha glances at me, tips her head, and then flits a longing look at Javen. Her expression churns a pinch of jealousy in my stomach.

I slip my arm around Javen's waist. "When are we leaving?" I ask Wirrin.

"Immediately," Wirrin answers. "Tensions are rising on the other side of the Intersection. And more of Earth's ships have arrived recently at your Skybase above the planet. I would like for you to get the potential

Intersection exploration over with as quickly as possible." Wirrin turns to Beda. "You'll be going, too."

"But—"

"Beda . . ." Wirrin's pale face grows stern. "You are one of the top warriors in this clan—"

"That's why I should be fighting with the others." She bares her teeth, reminding me of when she attacked me on the streets of Primaro. I squeeze my arm tighter around Javen's waist.

"No," Wirrin says. "It's why I need you here. I don't know how Cassiopeia and Dr. Foster fit into our futures, but I certainly don't want to see them dead. Both you and Yaletha will escort and protect her on the way to and from the Intersection point."

Great.

"Javen will go as well," he continues.

At least he'll be there, I sigh inwardly.

I stare at Beda and Yaletha. These are probably two of the most unlikely people to help make sure I stay alive. Beda hates me because I exist, and both aren't pleased that I'm with Javen.

"We should get going," Javen says. His calming voice releases the air from the ballooning tension in this room. He pilots me toward the exit and away from the others.

"I have something for you," Wirrin says, stopping us.

In Wirrin's fingers a Starfire crystal dangles along a length of natural twine.

My heart skips. "That's not mine from before, right? Hammond still has the one she stole?"

"Correct," Wirrin says.

Beda stares at the Starfire, eyes narrowed, but says nothing. Yaletha waits in a soldier stance, expression blank.

I take the crystal from him and place it around my neck. The gem glows and pulses in a slow rhythm.

Beda rakes her hands through her hair and turns away.

"You'll most likely need the crystal to have any chance of locating your father," Wirrin adds.

"Thank you." I let out a sigh. "You know, you are very kind." Something about Wirrin does make me want to trust him. Maybe he reminds me of my own father. I'm not sure.

Wirrin bows his head. "Kind is not something I've been called as of late." He shifts his attention to Beda, who quickly glances away from him. "You should begin your journey. Conserve the Starfire's energy by traveling on foot."

A few miles outside of Irilee, the terrain is reasonably flat and easy to navigate. But the trail is also entirely out in the open and leaves us visible from all sides. I peer around for possible attackers, who could appear at any time over the surrounding mountain range.

"Relax," Javen says, taking my hand. "Nothing is going to happen to you along the way."

I swing my head around to Beda and Yaletha, who walk fifteen feet or so behind us, and then back to Javen. Along our path, green grasses sway in the breeze, and the morning sun glows above us. "Wirrin sent them along for a reason. And neither like me."

"Their escort is only a precaution. Neither Wirrin nor my father will allow our people to harm you now."

"How do you know?"

Javen shrugs. "Because I know my father's desires for the Alku and the Starfire. Yes, my people have temporarily split over the choice to use the crystals as a weapon, but they don't wish to go to war with *each other*. A resolution will be found."

I stare up at Javen's handsome face. His square jaw is set with confidence.

I reach up and touch his naturally dark tan cheek, and from behind, Yaletha clears her throat.

"What's up with her?" I whisper.

A fraction of Javen's confidence falls from his face, and he looks to the ground. "She was my intended."

My eyes widen, and I fight the urge to turn and stare at Yaletha again. "Your *intended*?"

Javen presses his lips together and glances to me. "As the Luminary's son, it's our tradition to ensure a good match. My and Yaletha's intention was not set in stone but was likely. The Starfire had not bound us yet. We were waiting. But when I met you . . . circumstances changed."

No wonder she seems to dislike me.

"So, are all the Alku intended?"

Javen shakes his head. "No, the tradition is only reserved for a few anymore."

"Why?"

"Because I am in line to become the Luminary of the Alku when I turn thirty."

"What? Like the king or something?"

Javen chuckles. "Not exactly the king." He looks at me and blinks shyly. "I would become the leader of my people."

My mouth parts as my eyes widen. "And will your ascension still happen?"

"Of course."

"What about Yaletha?"

"She'll find someone else. I'm not right for her. I'm right for *you*." He slips his hand in mine and I feel the burn of both Beda and Yaletha's stares at the back of my head. I could be imagining it—but probably not.

Heaviness weighs on my chest. I have no idea what Javen's position as Luminary means for me—for us—for the future. *If* there even is a future for the Alku. My thoughts drift to the war playing out on the other side of the Intersection. Maybe if I can find my dad, he can help stop the madness somehow.

I squeeze Javen's fingers.

"The point is up ahead," Yaletha calls from behind us.

I crane my neck and see her pointing to a small grouping of short trees. My heart and feet pick up the pace. I hope to see my dad again. I drag Javen with me and stop a few feet in front of the first tree but then realize that I'm not entirely sure what to do. Every other time I've crossed the Intersection, it has just happened, or Javen has crossed me over.

"Are we all passing through together?" I scan the group.

"Yaletha and I are ordered to stand guard on the Alku side of the Intersection and wait for your return," Beda says.

"I'll go with you, though," Javen says.

Relieved, I look around at the ground, but there's nothing but dirt and grasses—no apples.

"Are you sure this is the right place?" I ask.

"Of course I'm sure," Yaletha snaps.

I open my mouth to apologize to Yaletha, but Javen jumps in before I can say anything.

"It's likely we won't be able to return to this exact point. But I'll open a new portal nearby. It'll take a lot of energy, but it's the best option to keep us together once we return." He looks to me. "Are you ready?"

I gulp in a lungful of air and push down the nervousness in my belly. "I'm ready."

I touch the Starfire Wirrin gave me earlier and grip my fingers around the crystal. Closing my eyes, I focus on thoughts of my dad.

Javen and I step toward where the Intersection point should be. Still touching my Starfire with one hand, I hold Javen's hand in the other. The space around us starts to warp and bend, and the air thickens, like water.

My heart slams against my ribcage as my mind spirals with fear and excitement. The space around us glows cyan, and I barely notice Javen's grasp slipping from mine until some unseen force snatches my body and rips me forward.

"Javen!" I scream, but he doesn't answer. Instead, the sound of a thousand lions roars in my ears.

My body twists and nearly rips apart. And then the chaos stops.

I gasp. Heaving in labored breaths, I turn in a frantic circle.

"Javen!"

The air is eerily quiet. The morning sun is gone, replaced by millions of twinkling stars. Arcadia's two moons still hang in the air, but this place is completely blue-green, as if no other color exists. Only shades of cyan.

Javen must still be on the other side. My shoulders relax and my fists uncurl.

Is the Intersection a whole other world? A planet of its own?

The grass sways in a cool breeze, and the blade tips glow. The lights form a path straight toward what looks to be a flickering fire at the base of a hill.

And I'm confident I know who it is. It's Dad. Waiting for me.

Chapter 3

follow the path that's lit by the tipped glow of grass blades until I reach the open mouth of a cave. Inside, the walls dance with cyan firelight from somewhere deep within.

I rub my sweaty palms on my pant legs and breathe out a steady stream of air from my mouth.

"Dad?" I call out, but there's no answer.

The hairs on my arms stand on end, but I step into the cave and walk about fifteen feet.

"Dad?" I call out again.

"Cassi?" Dad's faint voice returns to me.

Tears prick the back of my eyes at the sound of his voice. I break into a sprint toward the light, and as I round a corner, I see him.

My heart nearly bursts at the sight. He slowly rises from sitting on a rock, wearing the same clothes from the morning we planned to leave Skybase together on a shuttle to Arcadia. The same Connect, too.

"Cassi?" he repeats.

"I found you." Tears stream down my cheeks as memories flood my mind—a kiss on the forehead after bedtime stories, a bandage on a skinned knee, proud smiles after my first ballet recital when I was six. Mom and Dad never cared that I had two left feet and no rhythm.

I throw myself into my father's arms. Calming sensations spread through my body as a strong sense of safety overtakes me. I squeeze his frame closer as he does the same to me. His beard scratches against my forehead, the facial hair long and scraggly after not shaving for so long.

"I thought I was imagining you again," Dad says into my hair.

"No, I'm here," I cry into his shoulder. "I came for you. They found the apples you sent."

Dad pulls away and stares at me with knitted, confused brows. "Apples?"

I nod. "The fruits showed up all over at the Intersection point I passed through to get here. Wirrin found them and thought they could only be from you."

Dad lowers himself to the rock and runs fingers through his tangled hair. "Apples? Wirrin? Yes, I did give him a bag of them several years ago."

I take a seat beside him in front of the fire. "You did mean to send the apples, right? So someone would come for you?"

"I was thinking of you and your mother a lot while I've been here. But I didn't mean to send apples. The Starfire is so complex," he mutters. "I haven't studied the energy nearly enough."

Dad pulls out a large glowing Starfire crystal from his pocket. The gem around my neck lights up.

He stares at my necklace, and a confused expression washes over his face. "Wait. How are you here?"

"It's a long story, Dad. A lot has happened, and much of it isn't good."

"What did Hammond do?" He pockets the Starfire again.

"It's more than Hammond. The entire World Senate has split. A war is in progress on Arcadia over the Starfire fields."

Dad leans forward and places his head into his hands. "The Senate has no idea what they're getting themselves into. That's what I was trying to keep under control."

"The Alku are working to defend the fields," I add.

"The Alku? You know about them?" he asks.

"Yes, Dad. I know all about them. I know everything—even that you and Mom came to Arcadia."

A look of relief falls over Dad's face. "I'm so sorry we kept that from you."

I smile. There are so many questions in my mind. But it's not the time to ask. "That's not what's important right now."

Dad brings his hand to his forehead and rubs it, his brows furrowed. "The Alku revealed themselves?"

"Some of them. They had to keep Hammond from mining. But their clan has split over the fight, as well."

Dad breathes out a frustrated sigh. "That's terrible news."

My lips turn up into a weak smile. "But when you get back, you can help patch this up. Make everyone see—"

"Before I came here, I was working on a new plan to harvest the Starfire in a way that would not harm the Alku. I had told very few people yet. It was preliminary."

"I saw some of your plans for Renewal on your thumb drive. We can help heal Earth with the Starfire."

His lips curl into a smile. "You are a clever girl to find that. But Renewal has expanded," he says. "My team was working on the project before the *Pathfinder* even arrived on Arcadia."

"Expanded? How?"

"When we were studying the Starfire. Matt Owens, from my team, had a theory that, as well as using the crystals to heal Earth, we might also be able to harness the energy and create a portal to transport people through."

"Like the Alku do?"

"Right," he says. "But with the aid of a computer program." He brings out a small black device from his pocket.

"What's that?"

"It's the prototype. Matt gave the device to me before the explosion." Dad opens the back and reveals a Starfire crystal embedded among the electronics.

"Is that what got you here?"

Dad replaces the backing. "I remember Vihann transported me. But since he wasn't with me when I reappeared, my hypothesis is that his energy mixed with the prototype's program and I ended up here. Jonas and Abbot, the rest of my team, theorized that the Intersection was itself a place. They were right."

"Why didn't you use it to get out of here—to come back to me?"

"The electronics are shot. I need Owens's device and the data in my lab on Arcadia. I transferred the data after we arrived at Skybase."

I inhale sharply. "No way there's any data left in the lab at the Capitol building. Hammond has control over everything. And that means she knows about the device."

"Not that lab." He smiles. "I never trusted Hammond enough to keep all my sensitive information in a place she could easily access. I had a remote lab built for me outside of the city. Only the people I trust the most know about its location."

"Then let's go there," I say. "Compile all the data and figure it out."

I grab his hand and try to pull him up.

He rises without my help and pockets the device. "Cassi, I can't go."

I stare at him in shock. "Why? I think I can cross you."

Dad pulls away from me. "The Intersection is keeping me here." He looks at the Connect on his wrist and taps the screen.

"What? How do you know?"

Dad brings out the Starfire again, and this time the crystal glows twice as bright as before, illuminating the cave walls. My crystal begins pulsing once more and waves of energy pass through my body. I watch Dad stare at the crystal in his hand as his green eyes begin to swirl. Fear plunges into my stomach, and I suck in a sharp breath.

"Dad?"

But he continues to stare.

"Dad, what's going on?" I shout.

He tightens his fingers around the Starfire and drops his hand to his side. He cocks his head and looks at me until the cyan cloud dissipates in his gaze. Eventually his eyes return to normal.

"Dad, are you okay?" I wait for him to speak, biting the inside of my cheek.

"The Starfire here is different than on each side of the Intersection, stronger and more difficult to control." He thrusts the crystal into my hand and my skin burns. Everything in me wants to drop it to the ground, but for some reason, I can't. I won't.

"Take it with you. Figure out how to harness this Starfire's power . . ."

"How?" I ask.

"Just go back."

"Can't we just try together, now? I'm only seventeen—I can't do this on my own," I choke out, my voice wobbly with forming tears.

"No," he growls, and his lips pull back a fraction. My eyes widen.

But then he blinks his eyes hard, and his features soften. "No, I'm afraid doing so could trap us both here. You must leave and come back with help."

I stare at him, not knowing what I should say. Something about this place is affecting Dad—something about this Starfire. What if he's lying about not being able to leave and he simply won't? I look down at the crystal in my hand.

"I don't want this." I shove the gem back in his direction, but he clasps his hand over mine and gently pushes the Starfire toward me. "I already have one."

"The crystal fields here are different, more powerful—"

But that's what I'm afraid of.

"—You'll need this Starfire's energy to leave and get back here again," he continues.

How does he know this? What isn't he telling me? Pressure builds in my chest, and I fear I might explode with every breath. "I came here to bring you back!"

Dad drops his hand from mine and turns away. "You will. Just not tonight."

"But Dad—"

He taps his Connect again and mine vibrates on my wrist. "My Connect didn't work on Paxon," I say, bewildered. "Why is it working here?"

"They don't seem to transmit information out of the Intersection. Nothing happened when I tried that before. It appears as if they can pair with each other while inside this dimension, though. I uploaded the coordinates to my lab to your device." He turns and wraps his arms around me. "The Alku don't even understand what they have in the Starfire, Cassi. I need you to figure out this crystal's power and then come back for me. And when you return, bring an Alku you trust with your life."

"Javen," I whisper.

"If that is the one, bring them. But don't reveal much of what you found here to anyone. Even the Alku." He squeezes me tighter. "Close your eyes and focus. I will guide you back."

My heart races and I work to slow my breath. A glow forms around us. The space bends and warps, and the feeling resonates through both my mind and body.

I fall into Dad's arms, limp, as blackness devours me.

I draw in a sharp breath and throw open my eyelids and then squint against the light of the now nearly setting sun. It was just nighttime. How did the sky get light again? My mind swirls in a jumble of confusion.

"I have you," Javen's deep, melodic voice soothes.

My vision clears, and I feel his arms around me where Dad's were only a moment ago.

Javen brings his hand to my face and wipes moisture off my cheek.

I plant my feet and straighten with Javen's help. "Thank you, I can stand," I say and wipe the remaining tears from my eyes.

Javen loosens his grasp, allowing me to stand on my own. What did I just see? I try to make sense of the puzzle—Dad—but he's different. He's trapped inside the Intersection and wants me to return with more information about the Starfire.

My stomach clenches as a vision of Dad's swirling eyes comes to mind. The Intersection is changing him . . . but the change doesn't feel like the man I've always known.

"Well, what happened?" Beda says as she gives me a not-so-gentle push on the shoulder.

I stare at her, a scowl forming between my brows as sudden anger burns in my chest. My fingers form fists, and I squeeze and pump them.

"Stop it, Beda," Javen orders. "Cassi needs time to recover. You of anyone should know traveling through the Intersection is difficult before you grow accustomed to the dimensional waves."

I don't break my stare from Beda, whose irises now swirl. Of course, she stands her ground, too. Anger wells in me and I rush at her as if my body has a will of its own separate from me. I couldn't care less anymore.

Beda's nostrils flare, and a wicked smile stretches over her lips. She pounces.

Javen's strong arm wraps around my waist and whips me back against his chest with a thump. At the same time, Yaletha lunges for Beda and slams her to the ground. Beda screams and claws to get loose, but Yaletha pins her at the throat.

"Beda," Yaletha growls. "You need to stop this nonsense! You're not able to help us if you can't control yourself."

"Let me go!" Beda yells, thrashing and pushing to escape.

Yaletha keeps Beda immobile by pinning her down again with powerful, muscular arms and legs.

Javen spins me away from the scene, and I struggle against him, but it's no use. Javen is much stronger than I am and there's no way I'm going to win.

After several wild heartbeats, my anger leaves me and I begin to relax. Once I fully do, Javen lets me loose.

"What were you thinking?" he scolds. "Beda has the strength to kill you. There's no way you would come out of that fight alive. And she would be justified among my people since you attacked her."

I slowly look up at him, embarrassed for my behavior. I've never been in a fight in my life. The most experience I've had is watching ancient karate movies with Mom when we both couldn't sleep. And I have a strong suspicion the lessons in those movies would provide little help in this instance.

"I'm sorry. I have no idea why I did that." But the memory of the strange look in Dad's eyes gives me a clue. One I won't share with Javen. At least, not yet.

My own Starfire still glows, the necklace hanging down my chest, but Dad's Starfire is no longer in my hand. My heart jumps. I pat my pocket and breathe a sigh of relief. It's still here. Vibrating. I move my hand to Javen's chest, and an instant calm rolls over me. "Did you locate your father?" Javen asks.

"Yes."

"Why didn't you bring him back then?" Yaletha asks. "That's why we're here."

"I . . . I couldn't." But the confession perplexes me. I have no idea if I could bring Dad over to this side of the Intersection or not. He only told me the transfer wouldn't work. My head swims as information swirls around in a whirlpool of thoughts. I have no idea what is real or true anymore. I look up to Javen for an answer, but even he puzzles me. A sigh loosens from my tightened chest. Dad told me not to give the Alku too much information yet. Information he didn't fully qualify. Does this mean I shouldn't tell them how a whole other planet exists inside the Intersection?

Javen turns to Beda and Yaletha as he snakes his arm around my waist in a protective move. "Cassi needs more time."

"Fine," Beda says. "She can have plenty of time to think on the way back to town."

I wiggle from Javen's hold. "Before we leave, I need a few minutes."

He reaches for me again. "I'll go with you."

My back tenses and I back away as confusion clouds his eyes.

"Alone, Javen. I need to be alone."

Chapter 4

Without looking back, I walk away from Javen, Yaletha, and Beda. But the disappointed and hurt look on Javen's face burns into my mind as I make my way off the path and through the knee-high grasses. As I trudge across the field, the blade tips sparkle with what looks like electricity, creating a marked trail behind me.

Whatever. I don't care if Javen knows where I am. And if I'm honest, I probably prefer it. I have no idea where I'm going.

I look up at the craggy mountain range, and at the base, a large section of the earth glows. Swirling mist moves its way over the piece of land as the sun descends behind the mountains. The scene is surreal. Something you'd only see in a fantastical sci-fi movie—not real life. But nothing about this seems like real life anyway.

When I'm far enough away, I take in a long draw of air and settle down in a spot where the grass clears slightly. I bring my legs up and wrap my arms around them, clasping my hands. I touch Mom's gold ring on my finger.

"Mom," I whisper. "I need you to tell me what to do. All of this is way too much."

Most of me only misses her, but a tiny part deep inside is angry. At *her*. Angry that she left. Angry that she died. It's not right . . . not fair. But with a settling breath, I push the ridiculousness over how Mom could somehow control her death back to the far corners of my soul, where it belongs.

What am I going to do? There's no way I can leave Dad inside the Intersection. Something there is very wrong and changing him into a person he's not. Why couldn't we just try to cross over together? A part of me fears the answer. Maybe he actually wants to stay.

I sink my fingers into the earth beside where I sit. The soil is silky, and I run my fingers through the dirt and close my eyes.

Dad didn't want me to reveal too much about the Intersection to the Alku. All this information about the Intersection falls on me now, but I don't feel qualified to make a choice that could not only affect Dad's life but who knows how many other people—Alku and human.

The soil trickles through my fingers and back to the earth. I scoop the grains up again and allow them to slip through, over and over. I stare at the glowing mist in the distance, letting the flow hold my thoughts steady.

What would happen if Dad comes back, anyway? Would Hammond and her side of the World Senate attempt to kill him? Maybe he's safer in the Intersection for now. I release a soft groan and fist a clump of soil. Just when my thoughts start to make sense, they fall through the mist and swirl back into anguish once more. No matter what I do, he could die—whether I leave him in that strange dimension or bring him back. And I can't lose him again.

Light footsteps shuffle behind me and interrupt my thoughts. I clench the soil in my hand and squeeze as I twist my neck. Javen approaches where I sit, his arms crossed over his chest and a sad smile on his lips. A wave of dark hair falls across his forehead. My fingers relax their grip on the soil, wanting to touch his hair instead.

Dropping my eyes, I turn away from him and stare at the mountains again. Dirt falls through my open fingers, and I wipe the excess on my pants when the last loose grain sifts through.

Javen lowers himself next to me, and though I didn't want him there, an overwhelming desire to be with him tugs at my heart. As if he can sense my disorientation, he keeps a few inches between us and doesn't touch me.

"I'm not ready to go yet."

"I know, but I was hoping you might change your mind about not wanting my company."

I turn to him and, unable to resist, bring my hand up to his jaw. The feeling of the light stubble under my fingers sends electricity through my body, settling in my chest.

Javen touches the tips of his fingers to my hand and closes his eyes.

Real feelings or not, I want to be with this boy. Everything about him makes me feel safe—grounded.

"See that cluster of light at the base of the mountain?" he asks as he lowers his hand from mine and slowly opens his eyes.

I lean from him and return my hand to rest atop the soil and grass. "I was noticing the glow a few moments ago."

"It's a new growth of Starfire that began developing several months ago."

"So, the crystals just pop up at random?"

"After a while, old fields tend to lose their effectiveness. When that happens, a new field will begin to develop. This process isn't common, though."

The Starfire's glow is beautiful, almost haunting with how the ribbons of mist move through the crystals.

Javen looks to me. "Why didn't you bring your father back?"

I sigh. "He wouldn't let me. He told me doing so might trap us both there."

"Then what can be done?" Javen asks. "If I could go, I might be able to help. But something stopped me from entering. Whatever it was kicked me back to this side."

I touch the Starfire in my pocket. The crystal is different than the one Wirrin gave me and might cross Javen and me over easily. But do I want to? The memory of the strange look in Dad's eyes sends a shiver down my spine. If I tell Javen about the new crystal, he'll probably insist we do cross, no matter the risk. He knows how desperate I am to have my dad back.

"I don't know yet. Dad did give me some information to check into. I need to speak with a man from his terraforming team when I get back." I feel bad for not telling Javen everything. First, he deserves to know, and second, I need someone to confide in. But the fear icing its way up my spine holds me back.

"When you find out anything, you must tell me," he says.

More confusion stirs in my thoughts, and my legs twitch with the same restless energy running through me. "I will." I start to push off the ground. "We should g—"

"There's still time." Javen catches my hand and keeps me from standing.

"But it's going to be completely dark soon," I protest.

A soft smile plays across his lips. "The Alku have sensitive night vision, an ability that has developed over time among my people. And Beda already told you we don't sleep much. So traveling after dark is no issue."

I lower myself to the ground again and stare at the glowing Starfire in the distance.

"What was it like inside the Intersection?" Javen asks.

Dad's warning crashes against my nerves like a bitter, cold wave. Restlessness builds inside my chest and demands an outlet, demands to be set free. Every beat of time seems so uncertain. But right now, sitting here beside Javen, feels right.

I move to sit on my knees and brush a dark strand from Javen's eyes before cupping his face. I stare into his eyes and let everything I know about him flood every sparking nerve ending in my body. I've seen his past in my mind. I've seen his soul. My heart races as I lean into him and let my mouth crash into his. This is the *only* answer I want to give right now. I let go of all my questions and doubts. Any feelings that Javen and I are a mere manipulation of the Starfire and nothing more are shoved aside. My fingers trail down along his jaw and down his neck to rest on his chest, just above his heart. Every craving for him I set free to dance with my pulse in the grass. At least for a while.

He doesn't seem to mind.

And for the moment, neither do I.

Chapter 5

"You two coming?" Beda's flat voice comes from the darkness.

My arms fly off Javen's chest, and I'm on my feet in about one second flat, scanning the terrain for Beda. Javen isn't as hasty, slowly standing beside me.

I shouldn't care, but quick, nervous breaths rise and fall in my chest. I wrap my arms around myself and swallow back the coursing adrenaline.

"How did you not hear her coming?" I whisper, remembering Javen's sensitive hearing.

"I was paying attention to you." He shrugs. "Of course we're coming," Javen says to Beda.

The light of the moons illuminates Beda's face as she walks closer, enough that the scowl on her beautiful face is clear. A scowl that is deeper than usual.

Great, just what I needed, another reason for Beda to hate me.

I walk past her toward the Intersection point, not because I really know where I'm going but to distance myself as reality grasps me again. No more avoiding the inevitable by making out with Javen.

"Cassi," Javen calls from behind.

"She's right, Javen," I say without turning. "We've been out here too long. We need to get back to Irilee."

I keep my arms wrapped around myself to maintain a personal sense of security while I stalk through the sparkling grass.

I'd move faster if I thought I wouldn't trip over a rock or wild animal along the way. Unfortunately, I can still hear Beda's whispers behind me.

"You are being completely ridiculous and throwing away our traditions," she says. "Yaletha is a perfect intention, and you know it. A few weeks ago, that was your plan."

I peer over my shoulder slightly. Beda flicks her gaze my way and then switches to her native language to give Javen what must be a few more verbal lashings.

Their footsteps stop, and I twist around again, not wishing to get too far ahead.

Javen stands, planted, inches from Beda's face. "Speak English, Beda. Your father gave orders to you and everyone else that we are to speak in a way the

Earthlings can understand if we are in their presence. This includes Earthlings you don't care for. I have nothing to hide from Cassi, and you may not either."

My stomach wrenches painfully at his words. Are they true? There are too many feelings I'm hiding from Javen.

"You are making a huge mistake, Javen," Beda says. "Most of the Alku have. We can't trust these humans. They will take everything from us."

Beda spins from him, but he grasps her arm to stop her. She makes an almost hissing sound when he does it, causing a shiver to tingle in my chest.

"The Starfire is changing, and you know it," he said. "The humans are a part of the process. There's no way for us to stop this momentum. If the crystals want us to make a connection with the Earthlings, then that is what we must do. And a connection is what I want, too."

Surprisingly, Beda says nothing to this. Maybe she knows it's true.

"We need to move," I call out, hoping to break their tension.

Javen leaves Beda's side and strides toward me, his eyes swirling cyan in the darkness.

"You need to make amends with Yaletha," she yells after him.

Javen ignores her and comes to my side. He takes my hand and pilots me forward.

None of us speaks until we reach the Intersection point, and even after, the conversation is pretty sparse. Yaletha and Beda rush ahead, as if to make a point or something. I'm sure the women would only claim that leading the pack was their protective duty.

Javen squeezes my hand, and I gaze up at him.

"Beda is at least partially right," I say. "You do have duties to your people. Please don't let me cloud your focus or who you are as a person."

He stops us. "Cassi, I have *never* been clearer than I am now about my duties to my people. Why do you think I joined Wirrin's clan?"

"To be with me?"

He tips his head. "That's only part of it. I want the Alku to live—thrive. I truly believe this will be through a bond with the people of Earth. I have little say in the leadership of the Alku yet. Decisions are still up to my father and the Council, and now Wirrin with his clan. But I plan to set the example of the bond first."

A few minutes ago, those words would have terrified me, but there's something about the way he says them. Each word peals clear with beauty and sincerity. Javen really is a person I would want to be with . . . Starfire or no Starfire. He's the type of partner people dream about spending their lives with—handsome, kind, passionate, intelligent. And he cares deeply about me.

"But you do need to make amends with Yaletha," I say.

Javen glances down. "Yes, I know. I've already made plans to speak with her in private soon. I've waited too long."

"Tonight. You have to make amends with Yaletha tonight."

Javen nods.

"I plan to speak with Wirrin when we get back about a way we can set my dad free from the Intersection," I say. "I believe involving your uncle is the right choice."

"I'll go with you."

"No," I say, "I need to do this alone."

Javen opens his mouth to speak, but I cut him off. "*And* you need to speak to Yaletha. She made plans for her life, and now you've suddenly changed that. Leaving her without a heart-to-heart is unfair."

"Heart-to-heart?" Javen asks.

"An honest conversation." My palms begin to sweat. An honest conversation with Javen is overdue as well. But I'm still not one hundred percent sure what I'm feeling toward him is real. Dad's behavior with this other Starfire has only added to this confusion. He's clearly changing. Maybe being manipulated. I need more time.

We walk in silence for a while. Eventually, the glow of Irilee greets us, and within a few minutes, we're at the edge. Yaletha and Beda disappear into a structure, and I squeeze Javen's fingers, not really ready to let go.

"I'm going to find Wirrin," I say. "We'll meet up later."

Javen grazes my cheek with the tips of his fingers, and my knees nearly melt. He gives me a gentle kiss on my forehead.

"You know where you're going?" he asks.

I look around, still a little lightheaded from the kiss, and spot Wirrin's home. A pale blue-green glow shines from the windows as shadows dance about inside. "That one, right?"

"Yes. Wirrin should be inside awaiting the news. I summoned him and told him we were on the way through the Starfire."

"Thank you," I say.

Javen slowly untwines our fingers with a reassuring smile and then strides toward the same structure Beda and Yaletha had entered.

When I arrive at Wirrin's door, I pause before knocking. What am I going to tell Wirrin? I feel stuck between my loyalty to Dad's request and the uncertainty over whether he was in full control of himself when he made it. The Starfire belongs to the Alku. Their people used the Intersection as a portal long before we built Primaro. So why shouldn't they know the truth about the crystal's power? What right do I have to hide any information from them?

I rap on the wood and a muffled male voice says, "Come in," from the other side.

Taking in a settling breath, I push open the large door, cringing when the hinges creak.

Wirrin sits at a small table in the corner with an empty chair across from him. Scattered over the table are two plates and several carved bowls of steaming food. The meal's aroma meets my nose, and I close the door behind me.

"I thought you'd be hungry," Wirrin says as he picks up a spoon, scoops from one of the bowls and places the mixture onto his plate.

My mouth waters and my stomach releases an appreciative growl.

"Take a seat." Wirrin gestures to the empty chair opposite him.

I lower myself to the wooden chair. With each strained inch, my feet begin to sting and my muscles quiver. The walk to the Intersection point and back was far longer than I'm used to trekking. But I ignore the burn and instead reach for the spoon in one of the bowls and serve myself a vegetable dish, one that looks similar to the one Beda provided before we left. The green, savory concoction smells even better than the last time.

"So," Wirrin begins, smoothing his white hair away from his pale face. "Did you find what you were searching for at the Intersection point?"

I stuff a spoonful of the food into my mouth to earn a few additional seconds to think through an answer. Wirrin simply leans his elbows onto the table and waits. I swallow the vegetables after a few extra chews than I'd typically do and then clear my throat.

"Well, obviously my father isn't here—so, not exactly." I remove the Starfire necklace he gave me from around my neck and place it on the table. I don't need it anymore.

"But was he there?" His eyes go to the necklace and then back at me.

"In the Intersection?"

Wirrin nods.

"Yes," I admit and then take another bite of food.

"But you don't want to tell me about it." He stands and clears his plate, leaving his uneaten meal still piled high, and takes it to the counter in the kitchen.

I set my spoon down so I'm not tempted to stuff my mouth again. "Honestly, I'm completely confused by what I saw. My dad *was* there, but he wouldn't come back with me." I bring my hand to my pocket, feel inside for the Starfire and pull it out. When I open my palm, the crystal glows in a more vibrant hue than any Starfire I've seen before.

Wirrin's brows rise at the illumination's intensity, and for the briefest second, his eyes swirl with cyan before returning to their normal shade of brown.

"I thought he may not return."

I scoff. "Then why did you even send me?"

"I needed to know the truth for myself. I've heard rumors about the Starfire from the Intersection." He returns to his seat, still staring at the crystal in my hand.

"Rumors?" I ask.

He shrugs. "Ancient stories about the energy these specific Starfire hold. The crystals, like the one you hold, are 'Mothers.'"

"Mothers?" I ask.

"These crystals are the source of the Starfire we use for life on the Paxon side of the Intersection, and the ones on Arcadia, as well. Almost as if the Starfire on each side is the life-giver to those on the other. Each has its own strengths and weaknesses."

"But each is dependent on the existence of the other?"

"Yes, exactly. But the Starfire you now possess is not. This crystal holds the power of both sides in one."

I open my palm again and stare. The gem's light pulses in my hand. "But that's good, right?" The question brings me hope that my father's situation isn't as dire as I once believed. Maybe I was seeing things.

"In theory, yes. But very difficult to control for us as fallible beings."

My heart sinks.

"The story goes that before we knew anything about the Starfire, a few privileged Alku in ancient times came upon these Mothers. The gems were beautiful and fascinating. And the possession of a Mother brought wealth, notoriety—power. And, in time, also brought jealousy, and then war. The owners were consumed, and everyone wanted to take the crystals."

My jaw tightens at each of his words.

"When the Alku had nearly destroyed each other for the Mothers, it's said that there was only One Pure Soul left. He devised a plan and stole all the crystals. Then, when he had them all, he journeyed far and hid them away. After this, each side began growing the Starfire fields as we know them today. Forever separated but necessary for each other. After this, the Alku's eyes were open to their mistakes, and we decided never to use the Starfire for evil."

"Did the One Pure Soul ever return?"

"No," he says. "But the tales say he fights to this day to keep the two Starfire types from joining again."

"But that's just a story, right?" I choke out.

"There are always truths in the ancient tales. Whether the events happened exactly as told or not."

I stuff the gem back into my pocket and wipe my sweaty palms on my pants.

"Your father? How did he appear when you met with him?" Wirrin asks.

"Um . . ." The words I want to say twist through my head. Do I tell Wirrin about Dad's strange behavior? Confusion wracks me.

"He was affected, wasn't he? Did he say why he would not return with you?"

I stay silent for a moment. "He told me he couldn't. He didn't want to risk us both getting trapped."

"And did Javen accompany you into the Intersection? Did he see your father?"

The memory of Javen being ripped from me surfaces and my breath hitches. "Javen tried but we were separated, and a force prevented him from crossing. I ended up there alone. When I found Dad, he wasn't the same. In some ways he was, but in other ways not. There was something *off* about him."

Wirrin sighs. "If the story is right, it is possible the Alku may be able to enter the Intersection, but as of now, we can only pass through to the other side. The Starfire within the Intersection may be preventing our access. But with the introduction of humans, circumstances may change. Until we understand more, you should not return to your father. There is already a war waging on the Arcadia side of the Intersection; we cannot afford to bring all-out war to this side, too. The knowledge of this place risks everything."

"But I can't leave him to die."

"I fear if you bring him across, we might *all* die. If he has been exposed to the Mother Starfire since the accident, we do not know what he might become or what has already consumed him. And if he comes back, I'm unsure if he will be able to resist telling other humans or using the crystals for evil."

I push aside my plate, no longer hungry. "What am I supposed to do then? What do I tell Javen?"

Wirrin leans in and lowers his voice. "You will tell Javen none of what we spoke of. Not until I have the chance to speak to my brother."

"And what do I do with this?" I rip the crystal from my pocket and shove the glowing gem in Wirrin's direction. The glow lights up his face from below as if we were sharing horror stories. Maybe we are.

Wirrin pushes my hand away. "My guess is this Starfire is a key into the Intersection. Otherwise, Dr. Foster would not have given it to you."

"You take it." I hold the gem out to him again, but he leans away from me.

"I cannot. For some reason, this particular crystal has bonded to you and you only. If I try to take it, the Starfire will only find its way back to you. What is set in motion will continue."

Chapter 6

leave Wirrin's home, my heart heavy, and gaze up as the door closes. A shooting star launches across the night sky, looking as if the trail is brushed with a streak of glowing cyan paint. In the past, seeing such sights would bring me hope and wonder. But I'm not sure much is going to inspire me after today.

I sigh and bring my attention to Irilee and then the Alku who mill around the main road. Most of them have merely ignored me since I arrived, but a woman with her child in tow stares and then glances away when she sees I notice her. I force a smile.

Wirrin told me to go back to Beda's home and rest for the night. I didn't want to argue with him, but there's no way I'm going back there. Yet, I'm not sure I want to talk to Javen right now, either. I know what will happen—the effect he has on me. And right now, I need to be alone with my thoughts, not clouded by our bond.

"Cassi." Javen's voice comes from behind me.

I turn, and when I see him, the thoughts I had a second ago suddenly seem foolish. Javen is safe. He cares for me—why wouldn't I want to be secure in his arms? Compelled, I sprint toward him and tears begin to slip down my cheeks. Before I know it, I'm wrapped in his strong embrace. The world may not be right again . . . but he is.

"What happened?" he whispers into my ear while his hands bury into my hair and draw me closer against his chest.

I want to tell him everything but know I can't. I pull away and force myself back into control.

"When will we be able to release your father? Were you able to make a plan with my uncle?"

"I've decided we can't bring him back," I lie.

"What? But you told me that was what you were going to speak with Wirrin about."

"For now, Dad is safer where he is. Hammond and the World Senate believe him to be dead, I'm sure. Bringing him back makes him a target."

Confusion sweeps over Javen's face. "But why did you change your mind? Is Wirrin forcing you?" He turns toward Wirrin's lodging and takes a step in that direction. "I can speak to him."

But before he gets any farther, I clasp his arm and stop him.

"This is *my* choice. We need more time to fully protect my father, and I need to find out what's happening on the Arcadia side of the Intersection before any rash choices are made. Wirrin agrees with the idea."

Javen runs his hand over his forehead as if attempting to work out my change of mind. "All right," he says after a moment. "But please don't wait too long. I believe you'll regret doing so."

"I agree." I study the ground. "I'm going to Beda's home to rest." It's not where I want to go, but if I don't tell Javen something, I'm sure he'll try to stay with me.

Javen nods. "She's gone anyway. Took a scouting party out and shouldn't return for quite some time."

"It's been a very long day. How about you walk me, and then I will meet you again in the morning?"

He brushes my cheek with the tips of his fingers and I lean into his touch, closing my eyes.

"The morning is a long time from now," Javen whispers. "But I want you to receive the rest you need." He presses his lips lightly to my forehead and leads me to Beda's without any more questions.

Inside Beda's home, the embers in the corner fireplace still glow red-hot as if she only recently left. I plop into a chair and stare at the gentle, pulsing glow of the dying fire.

Weight from my new knowledge presses on my chest and I pull the brilliant Starfire out from my pocket. How can this small crystal represent so much power? Enough to nearly bring down a civilization? And from what I've seen, the Alku are better than many humans. Even though Wirrin and Vihann are split, they are still on speaking terms and wish to join together again at some point. On Earth, it's never-ending separation and trying to take power from the weak. Humans come to Arcadia, and we do the exact same thing in claiming the land and Starfire without thought to the consequences to anyone or anything already here. Dad was always the voice of reason and a friend to the Alku. How can we leave him out of this? It's not right. We need his presence to help solve the rift.

I squeeze my fist around the Starfire, and the gem begins to pulse in my hand. I squeeze tighter and press my eyelids closed with nearly the same force. I grit my teeth in frustration and the crystal begins to vibrate. The sensation spreads from my fingers to my arms and then races through my body. I inhale deeply and flick my eyes open to find the space around me warping and bending. I jump to my feet, and in a single blink, I'm not in Beda's home anymore.

Rather, I stand at the mouth of the same cave Dad used as a shelter. My heart pounds as I touch the rough opening and realize this is real. I've brought myself inside the Intersection again.

But instead of night, like the last visit, the light appears to be midday-bright. I turn my neck and squint at the sun high in the azure sky.

I enter the mouth of the cave even though Dad may not be inside. He could be doing anything during the day—getting food or water, searching out the crystals to study.

My heart thuds against my ribcage as I follow the cave walls, creeping forward until I arrive at the open section I found Dad in before. I spot movement to my left. It's Dad, hunched over a small, wooden table with peeling paint. Where the table came from, I have no clue. It wasn't in here last night. He's muttering to himself, but I can't hear what he's saying. Dad doesn't see me and grabs an object off the table and clenches his hand tightly while whispering to the air.

Fear ripples through me. But I must speak to him. "Dad?"

He doesn't answer and continues fiddling with the items in front of him, including a few Starfire crystals, which dimly illuminate the cave. A small amount of light from the outside also spills around the corner.

This time, I raise my voice. "Dad!"

With a jerk, he stands from the stool he's been sitting on. "Who's there?"

"It's me . . . Cassi." I want to go to him, but my feet remain frozen. What if Wirrin is right?

He squints and leans forward at the waist. "Cassi?"

"Yes." I force my feet to go to him.

"What took you so long?" He plops into his seat and returns to sorting though his items.

As I step forward, I see several of the items are relatively primitive tools, but there's also a pencil and a pad of paper with scribbles and notes all over the open page.

I step closer to him and he pulls the notepad away as if he's attempting to hide his notes. "Where did you get all this stuff?" I ask.

He grabs the pencil and begins scribbling in his notepad. A few seconds later, he puts it down. "After you told me how I had manifested the apples outside the Intersection on accident, I tried to make something like that phenomenon happen here—on purpose. At first, nothing happened. But the more I tried and the more I studied the crystals, I was able to make a few small things appear—food, tools I needed—even a pencil and paper to record all my findings. Nothing more complex than that." Dad bites the pencil and holds it in his mouth. He begins flipping back in the notepad to the beginning. He reads whatever he has written, looks up at me, and then removes the pencil.

"Why haven't you brought an Alku here, like I asked you?"

"Um . . ." It's not a question I really want to answer. "I don't know how yet."

Essentially, it's true, and I don't need to tell him how I don't want Javen to come here right now, even if I could get him here. Not until I know more about this place. What if the story Wirrin told me is true?

"You couldn't have figured it out by now?"

"Dad, it's only been a few hours."

His shoulders drop, and his body relaxes. His demeanor almost returns to normal, but then he rubs his head in confusion. "Oh yes . . . I've forgotten already. It feels like days."

"I'm not even sure how I got here this time," I say. "I was studying the Starfire you gave me and here I am."

He places his notepad down and stares at me. "You mean you didn't need a set point to enter?"

Dad grabs the pad and flips to a blank page. He jots down something while mumbling a few sentences to himself. He returns to hunching over the tabletop as if I'm not even here anymore. I watch him slipping from me again for a few moments before I say anything.

"Dad?"

He looks up startled. "Oh . . . you're still here?"

"Dad." I race to the other side of the table and kneel in front of him. "What is happening to you? Do you even know? We have to figure out how to stop this . . . change."

Dad answers with a blank stare, and just when I think he might come back to me again, he returns his frantic attention to the notebook, touching the Starfire on his left with his free hand. The crystal glows and his body relaxes.

My heart pounding, I rise, and he continues to ignore me. There's no way I can bring him back like this and I can't leave him here either. Wirrin was right.

I need to return to the Arcadia side of the Intersection. The World Senate really does have no idea what they're dealing with in the Starfire. I don't even know if I should be using the gems. Who knows what the long-term effects of the crystals are on humans? Even the less-powerful crystals from outside the Intersection.

I pull the small gem from my pocket and turn it in my fingers. The cuts are delicate and perfect. But could the Starfire still affect me in the same ways it's changing Dad if I keep the crystal for too long? I think about the One Pure Soul and how he had to take all the Mother Crystals to keep the Alku safe. I stuff the gem back inside my pocket. If this Starfire is my key to get back to Dad, then I must keep it. Reluctantly, I step away and watch him disappear into his own world again.

"As soon as I can, I'll get back to you, Daddy."

My heart aches, and I slip my hand into my pocket and close my eyes.

When I open my lids, I'm in Beda's chair, the smoldering embers still beside me in the fireplace.

A sound in the shadows makes me jump and my breathing picks up as I see Beda's outline in the kitchen. Why is she here? Javen said she was out scouting.

"Where were you?" She holds up a knife and then opens a drawer. I gasp at the sight.

I must have just appeared out of nowhere in the seat. But this sort of thing must not be an infrequent occurrence for Beda.

My quick breathing returns to normal as she puts the knife away in the drawer instead of directing the sharp point at me. Not that she needs a knife to hurt me, though.

"Beda, I must go back to Arcadia."

I ignore her question, but I'm pretty sure she might like what I'm telling her better. She raises her eyebrow in interest. Apparently, I was correct. But then her brow lowers and her face twists into a suspicious expression as she utters one word.

"Why?"

"There are things to take care of. People I need to see, starting with the Board members, Hirata and Cooper, then my Dad's lab partners." What was that guy's name again? Dad mentioned him. Oh yes, Owens.

"I can't do that from here. Keeping me hidden in Irilee isn't going to do the Alku any good if I have information people need to help stop the war."

Beda walks out from the kitchen and crosses her arms over her chest. "Well, I have no problem with you leaving. It was definitely not *my* decision to have you stay in my home. I'm not sure what my father was thinking." She narrows her eyes to slits.

My heart thuds as she continues toward me, stopping only a foot away to tower over my head. "But you need to make sure when you are over there that you do nothing . . . *nothing*"—she growls with an emphasis on the last word— "to harm my people, including my family."

I press my back into the chair to move away from her. "I don't think you understand, Beda. I have no desire to harm anyone . . . human or Alku. I want to rescue my dad and find a way for both our people to live in peace. Nothing else."

"Nothing else? What about Javen? Where does he fit into this whole grand plan of yours?"

"Javen?"

"Yes," she hisses. "Javen. What do you want from my cousin? Power? Position?"

"No," I protest. "I don't want any of that—"

"Then what do you want, human? Because power and position are what come with Javen eventually. He will be the leader of our people. How will you fit into *that* picture? Because I for one won't see you as the intended to the Luminary of the Alku. And many others will not, either." As she spits her words at me, she moves in closer, baring her teeth under her full lips. "And if you jeopardize Javen's ability to take his rightful position, I'll personally ensure that your Starfire connection is severed."

"Severed?" I ball my hands.

"Yes." She sneers prettily and then huffs a disgusted laugh. "Didn't know that could happen, did you? The connection is a binding force but not unbreakable."

Uncurling my fists, I gently shove her back. "Get away from me, Beda."

She throws up her hands shoulder high and backs away. "I'll speak to my father about returning you tomorrow. But I'm sure he'll agree." She turns and walks out the front door, leaving me alone.

I lean forward and shove my head into my hands. Where *do* Javen and I fit into all of this?

blink my eyelids open to the morning light streaming through the window in Beda's home. My body aches all over. I apparently slept in her chair all night. Guess the Starfire hasn't completely changed how I need a full night's sleep yet.

I roll my neck to work out the kinks. Memories of my second visit to Dad and Beda's conversation with me—if you can call it a conversation—turn through my mind.

Guilt stabs at me for having to leave Dad in the Intersection. But I'll get help in figuring that out. I just hope I'm able to before it's too late and the Intersection changes him beyond repair. I glance down at my rumpled and twice-slept-in shirt and black pants. I can almost feel the tingly spray of hot water on my skin as I dream about a shower once I return to Arcadia, as well as the comfort of a fresh change of clothes.

A rap echoes at the door and my breath hitches. Probably Beda again. But why would Beda knock on her own door? And it's not as if she gives me my space or privacy.

I walk to the door and open it. Outside stands Javen, looking fresh and clean compared to me. But Javen gives me a soft smile and doesn't seem to care about my disheveled appearance.

"You're going back?" he says, his voice peppered with sadness. He steps inside and shuts the door behind him.

Beda must have already spoken to Wirrin and told Javen my news.

"I need to. Staying here is useless. And there are things going on that you're not aware of."

"Then tell me. Right now, I'm left out of all the decision-making. You are not telling me everything . . . Wirrin isn't telling me everything. The war is driving a wedge between the Alku."

I turn from him and walk toward the living area. "You are the one who convinced Wirrin to use the Starfire as a weapon to drive Hammond out of Primaro."

Javen stares at the floor, then pinches the bridge of his nose. "Because I felt it to be a temporary, emergency solution. But I feel the shift of my people inside me—a shift toward more war—and I can't let this rift happen."

"Am I holding you back?"

Javen looks up, startled at my question. "What? Why would you ask that?"

Tears sting my eyes. "Because it might be true. What if our connection is actually dividing you? How are you supposed to stay loyal to the Alku and loyal to me . . . a human?"

Javen furrows his brows. "Cassi, you are a part of who I am. There's nothing that can change that now."

But there possibly is. What if Beda is right and severing my connection with Javen is the right thing to do? Sometimes I fear that I'll hold him back from stepping up to become a leader for his people.

I push away the thoughts. If humans and the Alku are to stay on Arcadia, our races need to make a bond. What better way than to set the example? As I study Javen's hurt expression, my need for him comes flooding back and all my doubts wash away. Javen and I are in this together, and we need to set things right as a team.

"I'm sorry," I say and step toward him. "The pressure is getting to me." I gesture to the room with my hand. "And staying at Beda's isn't helping the situation. She keeps freaking me out."

As he has before, he opens his arms to me and I fall into them. His warm, muscled chest feels good against me and, for a moment, helps me forget the mess.

"My dad isn't okay," I admit into his chest.

He leans away from me, and I look up to him.

"What do you mean?" The corners of his mouth tilt downward.

"He gave me a Starfire when I saw him yesterday. And last night the crystal took me back to him."

"From where? An Intersection point?"

"I don't think so, unless the Starfire created a new one. I was here in the living room, and then I was there—in the Intersection."

"So, you were able to create an entrance point leading inside the Intersection on your own?" Javen furrows his brow. "How could that happen?"

"I have no idea how it's working, but before a few weeks ago, I didn't know two dimensions could exist on the same planet. So at this point, anything seems possible."

Javen reaches for me and gently takes my hand. "Then what's next?"

"I need to go to Arcadia and contact some of the people from Dad's terraforming team. He trusted them."

"How is his team going to know how to help you? How much could they know about the Intersection?"

Frustration brews in my stomach. Dad said they were working on a theory that the Intersection was an actual place, and Dr. Owens did make the device Dad had that may have allowed him inside the dimension. So they might know something. "I need help from someone. And the ousted World Senate members must have people on Earth who can do something." I search Javen's eyes.

"I'll go with you," Javen offers. "I can be a liaison and help answer questions as best I can about the Starfire. Maybe my information will help the willing Senate members take action more quickly."

"But your people need you here."

"I know, but maybe on your side I can find out information beneficial to both of our people. And find a way to stop using the Starfire as a weapon. Maybe there's a way to use the power for good."

I nod, but in my heart I know the World Senate and Hammond have their own weapons. And I doubt whether, without using the Starfire as our own weapon, we'll be able to hold them back.

Chapter 8

As I take Javen's hand electricity ripples through my fingers and arm. As the space around us warps, a warm sensation of safety falls over me, just by having him here. I want more than anything to completely give into the feeling. But something tickles at the back of my mind, warning me to stay alert, to be on guard.

With a snap, Javen and I go from pure, organic surroundings to streets and buildings. A dull cyan glow surrounds us. Javen has us cloaked from view. So I keep hold of his hand to maintain our invisibility.

A few of the buildings in downtown Primaro are damaged by the fighting, but overall the city is in better condition than I thought. Everything is still standing, at least. I'd hate to see all of Dad's hard work destroyed.

I tap my Connect, using my free hand, and select the mapping function. A hologram of our current location appears over my wrist device.

"Spectra, the restaurant I worked at, is only a couple of blocks away," I say. "I'm going to tell Max to meet us there if he can."

Javen flinches slightly at the mention of Max's name but bows his head.

I tap my Connect to message Max.

Meet me behind Spectra as soon as you can.

Almost immediately the words from my friend appear on the screen. My heart skips at the thought of seeing him soon.

You're back?! I'll be right there—10 minutes tops.

I pull Javen forward, and we weave around a squad of troops who have weapons slung over their shoulders. I glance back after we pass. They're all human, not a single Alku. A ship passes overhead. My shoulders flinch, but the vessel passes and only seems to be patrolling.

After two blocks, we travel through a walkway leading to the rear of Spectra and then wait. Javen leans his back up against the wall, still holding my hand. I open my mouth to speak when a group of people round the corner, cutting me off. Even though no one sees me, I press against the wall next to Javen.

The two men and one woman stop less than ten feet from us. The woman is well-dressed, with curly, dark hair pulled into a low ponytail. The men are equally well-dressed. I narrow my eyes. The entire group looks as if they work in the Capitol building.

"If mining the crystal ore is a way to save Earth, then we should do it," the shortest of the two men say. "We are talking about billions of people."

My heart sinks when I realize what the group is discussing. Primaro has been secured. Those who agreed with Hammond should have already fled. If the people who stayed behind are beginning to back her, we may be in real trouble. I watch Javen as he studies the group, jaw clenched.

"We should wait this out." The other man leans in and whispers. "I want to save Earth, too. Of course, I do. But we have no idea what these Alku people are capable of. Sure, they seem to be helping us for now. But the Starfire ore appears powerful. I wouldn't want them turning on us. You've seen those alien movies— if you know what I mean."

The short man grimaces.

The woman crosses her arms over her chest. "I've received access to the preliminary reports. The Alku are definitely holding back on the Starfire's capabilities. I don't trust them. And I agree we should take them out while we have the chance. They're not resisting. Why wait until they do?"

My Connect buzzes, and I turn my wrist over. Max.

I'm heading around the corner.

Before I have a chance to tell him to wait a few minutes so we can listen to more of this conversation, Max is already in sight.

The woman spots him and glances at her Connect. "I'm on my way to breakfast. Does either of you want to join me?"

"Sure," says the taller man.

"There's a meeting I'm due at in twenty minutes," the other man says.

They bid their goodbyes and leave.

Max jogs our way, searching around for us. My heart picks up the pace as he gets closer. I let go of Javen's grasp, and the cyan glow around us dissipates.

Max skids to a stop. "Whoa, were you there the whole time?"

"Yeah," I say and rush toward him, pulling him into an embrace. "Just being careful." My heart fills with joy at seeing him again.

Max lets out a sigh and then eases from me. He glances at Javen, who is staring intently at him, an eyebrow raised.

"Well," Max says, "I should get you two out of here. Things are pretty quiet right now and almost normal since the Senate called a truce. But word is that people are getting restless. I try not to be on the street unless I have to be. I brought a car to take us back to base."

"Is Irene there?" I ask.

Max snickers. "She's been taking over the place."

I chuckle. "Sounds like Irene."

I grab for Javen's hand again, but he backs up.

"I can't go with you," he says.

Confused, I reach for him. "Why not?"

"You heard those people, and he"—Javen flits a look at Max— "just confirmed that the people of Primaro are growing restless. I need to speak with my father and Wirrin about the conversation we overheard."

"But there'll probably be more information once we get to Hirata and Cooper. We can find out all the details about the World Senate talks."

A sad smile softens his face and he whispers, "I must speak with my family now. We are running out of time." He touches my cheek, and the lingering graze of his fingertips makes me gasp. On instinct, I raise on my toes and touch my lips to his. He returns the kiss passionately and locks his arm around my waist. Stars fill my pulse and then, like a wisp of air . . . he vanishes.

Max clears his throat from behind, and I spin on my heels toward him.

"Uh, sorry." My cheeks are strawberry pink now; I can feel the flush. "You didn't need to see that."

Max shrugs and studies the ground. "We should go."

I follow him around to the front of the building and spot the white car he must have brought. He taps his Connect and the doors slide open. Movement catches my eye and I watch another group of soldiers patrol the street. Apparently keeping the peace. I speed up to receive the protection the vehicle offers. I doubt it's any safer. Really, nothing out here feels safe anymore. Nevertheless, I let out a shaky breath of relief as Max slides into the seat next to me and secures our doors.

He runs his finger over the display in front of him and taps a few times. The car moves forward.

"It's really good to see you," I say.

Max sighs again. "It's good to see you, too. I hate the fact I couldn't message you while you were with the Alku."

"For some reason, the tech doesn't work across the Intersection."

"I'm still trying to work out all this Intersection stuff."

I laugh. "Me too."

"Well, you seem to have a better handle on everything than me."

"Trust me, the Intersection is still a mystery to me in many ways. I just hope I can find out more information in Dad's lab."

"His lab?"

"Apparently he had a secret lab built outside the city."

Max narrows his eyes while still watching the road. "Then how do you know?"

"My dad is alive."

Max opens his mouth in shock. "What? Where is he? That's amazing!"

"I can't tell you yet. Until I get more information, no one should know. I'm afraid exposing him could make him a target again."

Max furrows his brows and blinks. "Why?"

"All I can say is the Starfire and crossing the Intersection are far more complicated than anyone previously thought. He wants to stay where he is unless I can find help." It's a white lie, but I can't tell Max why I'm leaving Dad where he is.

"You must be relieved he's alive though, right?"

"I am. And I got to visit him twice."

"And he's okay?"

"Yeah," I say a little too quickly.

Max furrows his brows further. "You sure?"

"Yes, he's fine. I'll just be glad when all this is over."

The vehicle stops next to a checkpoint manned by armed soldiers. Max activates the window on his side of the car. When the guard sees Max's face, he waves him past.

"The building we're in has a lot of security, so everyone should be safe," he says as the window moves back in place. "But before the truce, there was an attack."

I peer out the front window and study the char on one of the nearby buildings. A smattering of plants growing up the side are partially burned away, too. More soldiers patrol the streets nearby.

The vehicle rolls into an underground parking structure and locates a slot to park in.

"Support for Hirata is growing," Max says as we exit the car and head toward the building entrance. "But there are still a lot of patrons and members of the World Senate who support Hammond. So, many of us are trying to stay off the common streets. Right now, a group of us are working and housed here. It's not as comfortable as I might like. But it's all right."

"And you said Irene is here, too?"

"Yep. You'll see her in just a few minutes." Max taps on his Connect as we approach a door. A hologram of Irene's face appears. She smiles when she sees him, her white teeth offset by her dark skin.

"Has the eagle landed?"

Max chuckles. "Yeah, I have her. Can you open the door?"

He swipes off the display and the door pops open. Max ushers me through. Inside is a well-lit hallway with white walls.

"This floor has been converted into sleeping quarters. Above us is where everyone works. When your dad had these buildings constructed, he apparently ordered them to be built into the ground. The area we are in now is nearly bomb-proof. I guess he knew there was a chance for war."

"Human habits seem to die hard," I say.

Max leads me up a single flight of stairs and into another larger hallway. We pass a partially cracked open door. Inside, a group of people works on computers and several others bustle around the space completing their tasks.

"Come on." Max waves me toward an open door about ten feet ahead.

I pick up the pace, and inside I see the back of Irene's dark hair while she works at a computer. A giant holographic screen wavers in front of her. On a computer next to Irene is a man, maybe in his sixties. I'm not sure. But he's partially balding and paunchy.

"We're here," Max says, and Irene spins in her chair toward us.

JENETTA PENNER

"You're okay," Irene says with a sigh of relief and stands.

I reach out and pull her into a hug. "You too."

She squeezes me. "Yup. But I'm stuck here with this rowdy group." She gestures with her head toward the man still sitting to her right. "Right, Howard?"

The man grunts but doesn't look up at her. Instead, he just keeps tapping his virtual keyboard and occasionally swiping at information on his screen.

I raise my eyebrow at Irene.

She smiles and glances at Max. "I need to get back to work. Why don't you give Cassi the rest of the tour and show her our quarters?"

"Are we still roommates?" I ask.

"Yeah," Irene says. "But don't expect the luxury accommodations we had before. There are two extra beds in the room, and I'm sure the higher-ups will move another roomie in soon."

I think back to our dorm room that was little more than a box and a tight squeeze for the two of us.

"Hey," Max says to Irene. "At least I've been able to give you a couple days of privacy."

Irene tips her chin at Max. "It pays to know people."

"Yes, it does." Max chuckles and looks at me. "Let's head out."

I start to follow him when my Connect vibrates. I raise my wrist, and an auto hologram plays. The same thing happens to everyone in the room.

The Board's symbol of Earth and Arcadia overlapping while surrounded by stars appears and then vanishes, replaced with the head and torso of a man dressed in a suit and tie. His hair is neatly combed.

"This is a broadcast announcement where we take you to Skybase and the recently adjourned World Senate gathering," the man says.

I lean in and ask Max. "What's this about?"

"The Senate was voting on a new President of the Board today," he says.

"They officially removed Hammond?"

"Currently Hammond is missing. No one knows where she is or if she's even alive."

My heart picks up the pace, and I return my attention to the holographic man.

"In a thirty-one to twenty vote, Lia Hirata has been named our next Board President."

Cheers erupt from outside the room we're in, and even Howard lets out a soft, "*Whoop.*"

"We were pretty sure she was going to win," Max says. "But this is great news. It means the World Senate is working toward a solution with the Alku. There have been rumors their leader even met with the World Senate."

"Vihann?" I ask. Maybe he's about to work this out peaceably. I wonder if Wirrin was there, too.

Max nods. "Yes, Vihann."

I look back to the hologram still playing on my wrist as Lia Hirata is sworn in. I guess they're wasting no time. She raises her hand to take the oath, and the camera pans back. It's then that I see him. A tall boy in a sharp suit, with hair falling just over his forehead. Keeping a serious expression, he reaches up to move the strands off his face.

Luca Powell.

Chapter 9

"Luca is with Hirata?" I ask, my chest tensing at the sight of him.

Max turns his attention to me. "Immediately after the Senate split, Luca showed up and surrendered to Hirata. He confessed how he was never on board with Hammond's plans but didn't have the power at the time to do anything to challenge her. Since he hasn't done enough for Hammond to remove him from the Board, he has pledged allegiance to Hirata."

My stomach churns at Max's words and my face must show my distaste.

"Look," Max says, "I don't trust the guy either. But Hirata and Cooper have spoken to him at length. And they do trust him. Enough, at least."

I glance at Irene, who's now watching us, and she mumbles under her breath.

"You can talk to them yourself tomorrow," Max says.

"Tomorrow? I was hoping to see Hirata today."

Max gestures with a tip of his chin to Hirata's swearing-in still taking place on the screen. "You can see she's a little busy today."

I sigh. But I guess this will give me more time to figure out how I can leave this bunker of sorts, get to Dad's lab, and then find Dr. Owens.

"Hey," Irene says, interrupting my thoughts. "You mind if I steal Cassi for a bit? I've been up for fourteen hours, and I could use a break. Then I'll take her down and show her our quarters."

"Sure," Max says and checks his Connect. "I have an appointment soon, and while I'm there, I'll confirm everything is set for you to meet with Cooper and Hirata tomorrow morning. First thing."

I nod as Irene takes my arm and pilots me out of the room, past Max.

"I thought you had work?" I ask.

Irene ignores my question. "So, what's happening on the other side?"

Whoa. That's a big question I'm not sure I'm ready to answer. Javen, my dad— the Alku situation.

"I don't feel like we're being told everything over here," she adds.

"I'm sure you're not," I say while thinking of my father's whereabouts. "My dad is alive." I admitted this to Max; might as well tell Irene.

Her eyes widen. "Really? I thought he might be from the video feed. Do the Alku have him?"

"Not exactly. But I need to get to his lab. I think there's information there I need."

"His lab?" Irene motions me through a door marked "Cafeteria." Inside, a few people sit at tables, and up front is an assortment of prepackaged, shelf-stable foods. We grab a few items to snack on and then glance around. "Let's go to our quarters," Irene suggests. "More privacy there."

She leads me down the stairs to the sleeping quarters floor and to a door marked "A-102." After using the thumb scanner, she opens the door and then activates the light.

The room is as sparse as Irene said, with only four cots and overhead lighting. Not very homey and way worse than the dorm ever was. Only one of the beds has been slept on.

"You can take whatever bed you want . . . except mine of course," Irene says with a smile.

I plop onto the nearest cot, and the bed squeaks as I do. With a resigned sigh, I open my package of granola and set my box of water down beside me. Every bit of tiredness and stress that I've been bottling up inside suddenly seeps through my body. What I would give for a shower right now.

"How is your family?" I ask, eating a bit of my snack while we talk. "Your aunt and cousins? Were you able to get a comm to them after everything went down?"

She purses her lips. "I did. I guess the World Senate was able to intercept your broadcast. The message never reached Earth . . . only the people of Primaro and the Senate know about the Alku. All outgoing comms are being monitored and delayed so that Earth doesn't panic from the news." She rips open her package marked Raspberry Protein Bites and pops a reddish cluster into her mouth. "I'm sure some information has gotten through. But it's not widespread yet. I was dying while holding back more info for her, but I knew my comm would only be deleted and I'd probably lose my privilege to send out any more messages. Everything is the same in LA, and my aunt was mostly just happy for the CosmicCoin deposit in her account. Helps take care of the rent."

I pause mid-bite for a second, stunned, before chewing once more. Earth doesn't know about the Alku? Or what bad shape their planet is in? I don't know if the lack of Earth's knowledge makes the situation better or worse. But I guess there's not much the people can do. Why stress them out more than they already are?

I swallow my bite and ask, "Extra Solar is still paying you?"

"No. Hirata arranged for me to start officially working for the Board. Pay is the same as I was getting before." Between bites, she asks, "So, you said your Dad had a lab in Primaro?"

"No, it's outside of the city. I'm not even sure anyone on his team knows the location. But there should be some of his research housed there. He gave me the coordinates. But I have no idea how I'm going to get to the location. On the way in, I noticed so many guards outside the building and within the secured area, and I'm not quite ready to tell Hirata about the lab yet. Especially not after seeing how Luca is on the Board again."

Irene grimaces. "I get that."

"I can't prove Luca is doing anything wrong. But I didn't trust him from the moment I met him."

Irene holds her protein cluster in the air, ready to take her next bite, but speaks instead. "What about that Javen guy? Maybe he could transport you to the lab, like he did for me out of the detention center."

"Javen is on the other side of the Intersection dealing with his own problems."

"Things not going well for you two?" Irene sits on her cot.

"What?"

"I was pretty freaked out that day in the Capitol building, but I'm not blind. I saw the way you looked at him when we were in there. When he was hurt." She raises her eyebrows at me as I say nothing. "You have big feelings for an alien."

My heart shudders. An alien? I haven't thought of Javen or the Alku like that. Aliens are little green men who take cows and unsuspecting people up to the mothership! But I guess he is an alien. That's what the man behind Specter called the Alku earlier. Or since the Alku were here first, maybe *we* should be considered the aliens.

"I do care for him. I think about him all the time. Feels as if we've always been together and shouldn't be apart."

"Sounds intense." Irene takes the last bite of her meal, and I'm only halfway through mine. "Really intense for a person you just met."

"I know. The Starfire has something to do with the connection. But I'm not sure where the Starfire starts and where I end."

"I've had to trust my instincts my whole life. Being a poor girl from LA, a lot of people tried to take advantage. But my instincts got me here. Arcadia may not be perfect, but without it, I'd probably be on the streets in LA, and my aunt and cousins would be, too. Don't let this Starfire be your number one guide. You need to keep that position. Trust yourself." Irene stands. "You should eat, take a shower, and rest. I have to get back upstairs, but after my shift is done, I'll come down here and we'll head out to find your dad's lab."

△ △ △

The rest of the day, I barely slept—maybe an hour, tops. But I was able to shower and change into a fresh shirt and jeans and tame the snarled mess my strawberry-blond hair had become. Irene even brought a few of my jewelry-making supplies, and I was able to affix the Starfire that Dad gave me to a necklace. But she didn't get Dad's thumb drive since the device wasn't in any of my things. Alina must have taken it. I touch my finger to the gem hidden under my shirt. It's still there. Could I just transport me and Irene to the lab myself? Without knowing more on how the Intersection Starfire affects humans, I want to use this crystal as little as possible. If we can get to the lab another way, I want to do that, even if getting there is more work.

"You sure you got enough rest today?" Irene asks.

"You're going to be a great mom." I smile and raise my eyebrow at her.

Irene scoffs. "I'm so used to taking care of my cousins."

I pull up the coordinates to Dad's lab on my Connect. "I slept fine. Feel good actually." The statement isn't a lie. I do feel great, at least healthwise.

"How long is it going to take for us to get there?" she asks.

"The lab is outside the city. Estimated time says thirty minutes by vehicle. You did get a vehicle, right?"

"I did." She throws a couple of water boxes and food packages into a bag and then slings the satchel over her shoulder.

I roll my eyes. Irene really is like a mother already.

"Oh, I forgot." She reaches under her shirt and pulls out a pistol. Before she lowers the gun, I see that she has a second one still tucked in the waist of her pants. Irene tosses the weapon to me, and I catch it.

My eyes widen. "What's this for?"

Irene furrows her eyebrows and her lips form a thin line. "You know exactly what a gun is for. But the question is, do you know how to shoot it?"

"No," I scoff. "Why would I know how to shoot a gun? Why would *you* know how to shoot one?"

"Lots of VR gaming." Irene whips out her gun and activates the laser power. She throws the weapon out in front of her, pointing to my left. "It's that easy. Ready and shoot." She lowers the gun, resets the safety, and then tucks the weapon at her waist. "But we should get going. I know the guard on duty, and he won't give us any trouble for leaving. The one coming on in twenty minutes will be more of an issue."

With reservations, I place my weapon inside my waistband as Irene and I exit the room. We head down to the parking garage. Ahead of us is a guard with dark skin and short-cropped hair. He smiles when he sees Irene.

"Hey, Trav," she says with a lilt in her voice I haven't heard before. Wonder if she's playing him or maybe she really likes him? "You got my quad?"

"Yep." Trav tips his chin toward an open-aired, off-road vehicle. "What do you need transport for?"

"Research," she says quickly. "My friend needs to get some organic samples. Hirata okayed the request."

Trav brings up the display on his Connect and gives us a thumbs-up. Whatever the screen reads must confirm what Irene says.

"Just one quad?" I whisper to Irene.

"All I could get, and you can ride behind me. We can deal." She turns her attention to Trav and smiles. "Thanks."

"No prob," he says. "But don't take too long out there. People are getting restless."

Irene pats the gun under her shirt. "No worries. We're prepared."

Trav green-lights us as Irene hops onto the quad. I sit behind her and show her the coordinates. She enters the numbers on the front display. The engine hums quietly to life as Irene starts up the vehicle, and then she turns the quad around.

"Maybe dinner tomorrow?" Trav says to Irene.

"Maybe," she says, and then we jet off toward the exit.

I lean into her. "You don't like him?"

"Oh, he's fine. But I don't have time for relationships now."

The gate to the exit opens and Arcadia's night sky greets us.

The quad's computer system takes us east, mostly off-road. But luckily the terrain isn't too bumpy. I'm aware the landscape is beautiful, but I barely notice. About two minutes out from our destination, I search ahead for what might look like a lab. But there's nothing. Just trees and underbrush lit by the moons. The quad slows, and Irene guides the vehicle under a tree and brings us to a stop.

"You sure you got those coordinates right?" Irene asks.

"Positive." I tap my Connect and bring up my Earthscape Lite program. Dad had me download the topography of Primaro and the surrounding area last year. I enter the coordinates, and a glow appears on the hologram. I line the image up with the real thing. Something is there, but I can't make out the specifics. "One hundred yards ahead. If the object isn't the lab, then I guess we're lost."

Allowing the quad to auto drive, Irene takes out her gun, but I leave mine in place and hope for the best. We follow the Connect's trajectory, and as we get closer, the blurred lines of a building become more evident. The lab's appearance is even more organic than the foliage-lined buildings in Primaro. This is more like the Alku's structures, blending almost perfectly with the surroundings. There are no apparent windows, only one door.

"So, I guess we're not lost," Irene says.

"Yeah. I knew my dad wouldn't steer me wrong." But the reality is I don't know.

We approach the front, and a palm scanner lights up next to the door. I look to Irene. Dad didn't say anything about the design.

"Try it," she says. "We came this far, might as well."

Gingerly. I place my palm on the scanner with the glowing frame.

The device beeps.

"Welcome, Cassiopeia Foster. Please enter."

My breath hitches as a shiver runs down my spine. Her voice. It's *Mom's* voice. Or, at least, a simulation. I remove my shaking hand, and the door slides away.

"Welcome," Mom's-voice-but-not says as we enter.

Lights with an odd cyan glow flick along the ceiling. They move in a forward motion, as if to guide us to a new location. This building runs on Starfire. Just like the Alku buildings. Dad built this structure entirely to imitate Alku homes from the outside in, except he integrated Earthen technology.

"I need to locate Richard Foster's lab," I say to the AI system.

"Follow the blinking lights," she says.

The lights flash in forward motion through the room and around the corner. Irene and I follow the path to a door, which immediately slides back as we approach. The inside room illuminates, and a youthful version of my mom appears in the middle of the space.

Chapter 10

gasp and take a step back, right into Irene.

"What's wrong?" Irene asks, lightly pushing me away to replace her weapon under her shirt. "It's just a hologram. We see them all the time."

I gape at the figure. She's not that much older-looking than I am right now. Her long strawberry-blond hair rolls over her shoulders and onto a blue, short-sleeved, collarless shirt. How I wish she were real. Ever so slightly, the hologram flickers.

"It's her."

"Her?"

"My mom." A tear rolls down my cheek, and I swipe the moisture off as quickly as I can.

"I'm so sorry. I had no idea." Irene touches my arm.

"How may I assist you?" the hologram of Mom says. She appears perfect, her brown eyes sparkling and awaiting any questions we might have. I reach for her, and my fingers cut through the image like a knife.

My stomach roils, but then I remember what we're here for—data on Dad's Renewal plans.

"I need access to Renewal," I say, my voice wavering just a fraction.

"Scanning voice recognition," Mom's hologram says. "Please be patient."

"I guess if this doesn't work, you'll need to hack into the system," I say to Irene. "If you can."

She throws her hand onto her hip, which must be her signature annoyed pose. "You doubt me?"

I chuckle, forgetting my sadness for a moment. "Not for a second."

"Access granted."

Data pops up on the computer display behind the hologram. But it's just a bunch of symbols, and I can't read the meaning.

"It's encrypted," Irene mumbles as she squints and studies the data. "We'll need to download everything and take it back. This project will take time. Not time we have here, since I scheduled us to be back an hour and a half from now. People will start searching."

"Can you download the data?"

"Already on it." She taps at her Connect.

I move my attention over to the false version of my mom. She looks so beautiful and so incredibly young, no more than twenty-five. She must be programmed to appear as she did when my parents were first married. I look to her hand and see the very same golden ring I wear on my hand. I touch the twin on my finger as more tears sting the back of my eyes.

"Seventy-five percent downloaded," Irene says, breaking me from my thoughts.

A beep emits from the display.

"What's that?" I ask.

Irene looks back at me and shrugs.

"Airborne vehicle approaching," Mom's hologram warns. "Arrival in one minute."

"Someone's coming," I say with a croak. "Is the download done?

"Eighty percent."

"Can you make it go faster?" I cry out.

"Doesn't work that way," Irene says, her voice full of frustration, probably at me and the download situation. "Maybe we should leave it. Try to come back later. I have no desire to be detained again . . . or worse."

"How much time do we have?" I demand from the AI.

"Forty-five seconds until vehicle arrival and approximately three minutes until lab entry."

"Can you identify the person?" I ask.

"Person unknown," she says. "Identity encrypted."

"Ninety-five percent," Irene says. "We're almost done."

"Is there another way out of the lab?" I ask the AI.

"Yes, but the rear exit is currently under repair and inaccessible."

My muscles go rigid as I try to think of what we're supposed to do. I pull the pistol out from under my shirt and stare at the shape of the gun. I don't really want to shoot anybody, especially when I have no idea if they are friend or foe. Can we hide? I scan the space, and it's possible. Several rooms comprise the lab. But I don't want to risk getting caught.

"Got the data. Let's go," Irene says.

I have no idea if what I'm going to do next will work, but it's my best chance. I look to the AI, my mother. "Power everything in the lab down including the lights. Do not inform anyone we were here."

"Immediately?" she asks.

"Immediately." I grab Irene by the arm and yank her next to me as everything inside goes dark.

"What are you doing?" Irene demands.

I don't answer her question but stick my gun back into my pants and grab for the Starfire hanging around my neck. I envision the space next to where we parked the quad and close my eyes. *Work! This has to work!* Electricity shoots through me, and a bright, cyan light bursts behind my eyelids.

I open my eyes outside of the lab. Right next to the quad. I push Irene and myself into a squat to hide behind our vehicle.

"How did you do that?" Irene whispers.

"I wish I knew." A sound pricks my ears. I lift a finger to my lips at Irene and then peer across the way. At the entrance to the lab is a man lit up by the hand scanner. I can't make out much other than how the light of the moon reflects off his bald head. He's short and has a bit of a belly.

"You know him?" Irene asks.

I stare for a moment, but I can't get a good look at his face from this far. "I don't think he knew anyone was in the lab," I say. "It's not as if he's in a rush to get in."

We both watch the man walk through the entrance, and the door shuts behind him.

Irene taps my shoulder. "We should get back before anyone misses us."

Reasonably sure the man isn't coming out, I stand and climb onto the quad behind Irene. We reverse the directions to Primaro and head back.

Questions swirl through my head about my parents and what the data is going to tell us. I hope we picked the right file and the AI version of my mom doesn't tattle on us.

△ △ △

We arrive back at the secured building before our time is up. Irene purges the lab's coordinate information from the quad, and then we return to our room. Irene heads in first and kneels on the ground in front of her cot. Reaching underneath, she pulls out a DataPort.

"Howard and I completely upgraded this thing. Looks like junk but it's pretty powerful." She taps her Connect to activate the device. "Give me a few minutes to get everything synced and uploaded."

I flop on my bouncy cot and wait. And wait. While Irene is totally engrossed in decrypting the data, I bring out my Starfire and study the cyan gem. *What secrets do you hold?* I graze my finger over the crystal. *Do you hold the key to Earth's salvation? Or are we opening a Pandora's box we'll never be able to close?* Of course, my hope is for the former. But only time will tell.

I tuck the gem into my shirt and a light shiver ripples over my body. I haven't experienced the sensation for a while, but I've decided my shifts in temperature occasionally have to do with my connection to Arcadia . . . or the Alku. I'm not entirely sure. At this point, I just accept the sensation as a part of whatever process is going on. I close my eyes, and a cyan mist settles over my thoughts.

And then suddenly, I'm not in the room anymore. Instead, I'm running through an open field, the wind blowing over my face, and I peer over my shoulder. A young girl is chasing me; she's maybe thirteen or fourteen. Her wild hair streams behind her. And she has the most beautiful face I've ever seen—Yaletha. I twist forward again, confused, and glance down. Mist covers the ground and dissipates momentarily as my feet pound the dirt. But they're not my feet I see. They're larger, a boy's. The moment I notice, my consciousness separates from his and floats away to hover over the pair. The boy is Javen. This must be Yaletha and Javen a few years ago. As I watch them run and laugh, an ache fills my stomach. Yaletha powers forward, catches up, and tackles him, and the two fall to the ground laughing. They sit up, and Javen brushes the side of her cheek, staring into her eyes.

Through my connection to him, I feel his longing for her. His excitement to spend his life with Yaletha as his partner.

Burning embers of jealousy flare in my core.

Javen leans in and kisses her lightly. Yaletha accepts the kiss and then pulls away, smiling.

"I can't believe we are intended," she whispers.

Javen takes her hand and raises it to his lips, kissing her fingers. Even as a younger teen, Javen was gentle and kind. He helps Yaletha to her feet and interlocks his fingers with the ones he had just kissed.

Tears slip down my cheek as the vision dissipates. The dull room comes back into view as intense sadness, jealousy, and a longing to be with Javen shudders through me. I inhale deeply and push the breath out. How can he not love Yaletha anymore when his feelings for her were so intense?

"Are you okay?" Irene asks.

"Uh . . . " I force my emotions back together. "Yeah, I'm fine." But I know I'm not. My mind is stuck in a place I don't understand when I should be focused on my Dad and how the Starfire can help Earth. Javen has his own issues to take care of that are more important than our relationship.

"You were out for a few hours, and I've almost got this data decrypted. I'm running one last program, and I think it'll clear everything up."

I was asleep for several hours? With a shake of my head, I stand and walk to her cot, now littered with an eaten prepackaged meal and its wrapper, as well as an empty box of water. She picks the trash up and moves it aside to make room for me.

"I think it's done." Irene scans the old-fashioned screen. "There. Now I'm syncing the file to our Connects so we'll both have the data. It'll be easier to scan through together this way."

A few seconds later, my Connect vibrates and "Upload Complete" flashes on the screen. I tap the device's face, and the hologram pops up above my wrist with the data. Irene does the same on hers.

The file is titled "Project Renewal," followed by Dad's name as well as a few others I vaguely recognize from his team. I had seen these individuals a few times, but honestly, they were always so busy with the Arcadia terraforming project that I never got to know any of them.

> *Dr. Matthew Owens*
> *Dr. Ann Jonas*
> *Dr. Grant Abbot*

An image appears beside each name. The one by Dr. Owens shows a bald man around sixty, and I'm almost sure it's the same guy from the lab. I tap the image.

"That's him," I say, pointing Irene toward the man.

She glances over and raises an eyebrow. "I think you're right." She stares at the image a little longer. "It was dark at the lab and I didn't recognize him. But now that I see his face, he's the same guy in the video feed your dad spoke to before the explosion."

The memory of the video feed floods my mind. He is Dr. Owens, the man who got Dad the device he still has in the Intersection.

Excited, I start reading, but most of the information is way beyond my understanding and full of terms I don't know.

"You getting much of this?" Irene asks.

I ignore her and do a search on the term Starfire and flip through the references. After what seems like ages, I finally get to a note that catches my interest.

> *Our team theory is that the anomaly the Alku call "the Intersection" is more than it appears.*

Yes, yes . . . I already know this.

> *We've done tests on a Starfire sample from each dimension, on both the Arcadia and Paxon (Alku) sides. The makeup is identical, but they are not the same. We believe there may be a binder inside of the Intersection, linking the two to create a much greater power source.*
>
> *Once we arrive on Arcadia, I'll be testing my theory. If I'm right, the Starfire's power inside the Intersection will be enough not only to maintain and protect Arcadia and Paxon, but also strong enough to bring a relatively small amount to Earth and regenerate the damaged atmosphere within a year. But first, we* must *get inside the Intersection to retrieve the crystals.*

"So, Dr. Foster was trying to get inside the Intersection?" Irene asks from over my shoulder while reading my display.

I blow out a nervous breath. "That's where he is now."

"What?" Irene asks.

"I need to find Dr. Owens. He still has access to the lab, so he might have more information. You think you or Max can get me out of here?"

I tap off my Connect and pop up from Irene's bed to change my clothes. Just as I reach for my bag, a pounding sounds at the door. I flit my attention to Irene, and she shrugs.

Just in case, I pull my gun out from my waistband and then inch toward the door and wedge it open a crack.

In the hall stands a wild-eyed Beda.

Chapter 11

"Who is it?" Irene says from the cot behind me.

"What are *you* doing here?" I ask Beda.

Beda pushes past me into the room. "Helping you." She drops a cloth bag she had slung over her shoulder to the ground.

Irene still stares at the warrior-like girl, uncharacteristically silent.

I shut the door behind us. "What do you mean 'helping us?'"

Beda whips her head my way. "Is there something about those words you don't comprehend, human? I'm speaking English, as I was told to do. Heeeellllping." She draws out the word and emphasizes the "p" with a pop of her lips.

For the first time today, I'm glad I still have the gun Irene gave me. Who knows if Beda might attack me at any moment?

Beda finally breaks our glare and scans the room, nose wrinkled. "Is there anything you can do about the smell in here? It's everywhere."

I plant myself, less afraid of her and more tired of her attitude. Mostly.

"Why are you here '*helping*?' Shouldn't you be on the Paxon side doing something—important?"

"Right," she grumbles.

"Knock off all this"—I wave my hand up and down in front of her— "attitude. Or you can go home."

Beda crosses her arms over her chest and narrows her eyes at me. "One problem."

"What?" Irene finally speaks.

Beda shoots a glare at her, too. *Welcome to the club.*

"Yeah," I say to pull Beda's attention back to me. "What problem?"

"I *can't* go home. The Council sent me here."

"To stay with me?" I demand.

Beda nods.

"Tell them I don't want you here."

Her jaw tenses. "Already tried. Believe me. I gave the Council every excuse I could think of. But tensions between my father and Vihann are growing, and there's distrust for the Alku among the World Senate. The other members of the Council recommended that one of us have a presence on this side."

"Because of your amazing personality? They thought you might sway people and help them understand the Alku?"

She bares her teeth at me and I shrink back.

Point proven.

"Why didn't they just send Javen?" I ask.

"Really?" she says. "Javen's Starfire connection to you is too strong for him not to be influenced. But they refuse to break the bond. Javen is distracted and may put you above the needs of our people."

"But why you? Your opinion of humans, or *me* for that matter, isn't positive or even neutral."

"No," she says flatly. "It's not."

But I know what she says is true. Even I worried that Javen would put me above his duty to the Alku. I pinch the bridge of my nose and turn from her just as the door to our room opens, allowing light from the hall to spill in. Max stands in the opening.

"Why are *you* here?" I ask.

"I messaged him," Irene says. "Told him to come right in. I figured you would want to share what we found with him."

Beda angles away from the door.

"Do you know about *this*?" I ask him and gesture to Beda.

Max nods. "But the instructions from Hirata just arrived. Beda is on your team now, apparently."

I let out a sigh. Great. Team Chaos.

"Then you are too, Max. And Irene," I demand.

"Done," Max says. "I already arranged it."

Irene packs up her DataPort. "I'll show Beda around the building and find something for her to do." She studies Beda, looking her up and down. "How about we start by eating breakfast?"

Beda rolls her eyes but agrees, and she and Irene leave Max and me alone.

I study Max and his ruffled hair. Apparently, his grooming hasn't had much attention yet.

"Did Irene wake you?"

"No, I've been up for a couple of hours, working."

I sit on my cot and lean on my knees, unsure if I'm able to handle this anymore—or life, for that matter. I want to go back to the time when I was sort of a normal kid. Not someone carrying a laser pistol in her pants.

"Max, I still don't really get why you are here . . . with me."

He looks around at the small space. "In your room?"

I roll my eyes. "No. Since the explosion, you've done nothing but stick by my side whenever you could."

Max lowers himself next to me and I instantly catch his clean scent. Like the soap he must have used this morning.

"I told you before on the *Pathfinder.* I've followed Dr. Foster's work for a long time. Every time an update was sent out about the progress of Arcadia, I was on it right away. And in the process, I got a little caught up in the stories released about your family. You see, my family was never close. It's why I immersed myself in work once I was old enough. And I told my father I wanted to travel on the first ship here. He agreed because my parents knew coming to Arcadia was prestigious and would look good for us.

"Are they still on Earth?"

"They had planned to come out in six months. But right now, the passenger ships are delayed . . . for obvious reasons."

"But why are you helping *me* so much?"

Max looks down. "Cassi . . . I've had a crush on you since the first time I saw you on TV."

His admission takes me aback, and I sit up. Heat spreads up my neck.

Max wrings his hands together on his lap and stares at a spot on the ground. "But I know you don't feel that way about me, and that's okay. I still feel like you're an old friend." He returns his attention to me, his eyes full of sincerity. "That's why I want to be here for you. I've been living the political game my entire life because of my parents. Might as well put it to good use. When I had the opportunity to work the Gala before we arrived on

Arcadia, I jumped at the chance. Never thought the shift would mean more than seeing you there— maybe meeting you. And when we did meet? It was like I had always known you. Sounds stupid, I know." He rakes his hands through his hair and blows out a quick breath.

My vision of Javen kissing Yaletha swirls through my mind. The memory tightens my chest. Max has been there for me at every turn. He didn't have to, but he was, and he's willing to keep helping me with unrequited feelings. I like Max so much. I have since the moment I met him at the Gala. I chance a look his direction and take in the rumpled blond hair, gray eyes, and the frown lining his mouth. A mouth that is normally always ready with a smile my way. Warmth loosens the knots in my chest and I relax a notch. I, too, feel as if I've known him forever, and I trust him completely.

Moved by his confession, I snake my arms around his neck and find his mouth. He gasps and tenses at my unexpected actions. Until now, even *I* didn't know that I would be kissing him. But in a snap, he relaxes and pulls my body close to his, as if he never wants to let go. I drink in the spicy scent of his skin and allow his kisses to engulf me. All I want is his strong arms and soft mouth right now. And my stomach flutters with excitement.

A clopping sound echoes down the hall and I flinch from Max's arms. The footsteps grow louder, and I know they belong to Irene and Beda—as if Beda needs one more reason to dislike me. But the steps continue away from my door. I let out a held-in breath and muster the courage to face Max.

A tense smile plays on his lips, the ones I just kissed. I open my mouth to speak, but he cuts me off.

"I know what you're going to say." He folds his hands and leans his forearms on his knees. "That was a mistake—" He glances at me and then away again. "Please don't tell me the kiss was a mistake."

I take in a long breath and gather my thoughts. "Max, I don't understand my feelings these days. Everything going on is so confusing. I was supposed to come to Arcadia and finish up school . . . make a life here with my dad. Nothing about Arcadia is what I thought. *Nothing.*"

Max tries to talk, but I hold my hand up.

"I liked you from the second I met you. Because you seemed kind . . . and thoughtful . . . and clever . . . and cute." My cheeks flush as I say these words. My mind is still torn. Since the Starfire revealed parts of his life through the visions, my ache for Javen has grown stronger through our connection. I've seen his past and present, caught a glimpse of the person he is—in his soul. And there's no doubt I need him. But how much of these feelings are real is the question. My feelings for

Max seem so much more organic . . . like I expect falling in love to be. Slower.

"A good personality isn't something you can fake for very long," I continue, "even if you did want to meet me because you idolized my dad or had a childhood crush on me. You didn't bail when life got hard, and it wasn't because of some crystal. I think it's because of who you are."

Max twists his head my direction and gives me a lopsided grin. Then the smile fades.

"So, what does that mean?" he asks.

"I don't know. But I am one hundred percent positive kissing you was not a mistake."

Max straightens. "So, should we try kissing some more, then?"

"I wish." I chuckle. "But right now, I need to find someone, and right away. Maybe you can help me?"

"Of course."

I proceed to fill Max in about everything that happened last night. How Irene and I took the quad out to the coordinates Dad gave me. I tell him about the AI version of my mother and that a man, who I believe is Matt Owens, showed up.

"And you were able to use the Starfire to transport yourself out of the lab at will—just like the Alku?"

"I've done it before, but I didn't know how." I think of the night Luca invited me to dinner and tried to kiss me, and I cringe. I only got away because I transported myself to Paxon—to Javen. My heart flutters with guilt as I think of Javen, but I push the feelings away and redirect my attention to Max.

"This time I focused on exactly what I wanted, and it happened."

"Think you could again?" Max asks, appearing to have forgotten all about kissing.

I contemplate the question. Considering what is happening to Dad, how he's changing, I have no idea if transporting myself is safe. Transporting multiple times caused Javen to deplete his energy completely. But the Starfire seems to work differently for the Alku than for me. They need to charge themselves with the gem. I seem to simply be able to harness the energy by having the crystal on my body.

"I'm sure I could make the transportation work again. But I don't want to overuse the power. Who knows what the long-term effects could be?"

Max nods. "And you have the name of your father's team member?"

"Yes, Matthew Owens."

He stands and holds his hand out to me, and I take it.

"Let's go find him, then."

I rise and gaze into Max's silver-gray eyes. Then I lean in and steal one more kiss from him.

Chapter 12

I t would be safer to transport. But Beda refuses since the ability should only be used in case of emergencies, and the Alku don't use the ability just because they can. But mostly, she can't transport all four of us without depleting her Starfire energy. In the end, as much as it annoys me to say she's right, I do. No vehicles are available. So, we walk down the streets of Primaro, each armed with a laser pistol under our shirts.

Since Hirata's swearing-in yesterday, tension within the city has picked up. People aren't happy that news of the war on Arcadia isn't reaching Earth. No one wants full-blown panic on Earth. But I think a lot of the travelers are starting to feel like cornered animals. And triggering fight-or-flight is never a good thing. Scared animals attack with little warning.

A group of people head toward us in a hurry. From their speed and intensity, I wonder if they're traveling somewhere important. Even before they reach us, I sense their nervous energy and avert my eyes. A woman, maybe in her twenties, has her gaze fixed straight ahead with fists clenched tight. As she passes, her shoulder collides into Beda's. Fire lights in Beda's eyes and Irene snatches her arm before she has the chance to say or do anything stupid. The other woman says nothing and only moves on.

"You behave," Irene growls. I smile inside at her scolding. Irene is like a mother to everyone.

Beda tenses but surprisingly relents—mostly. "Humans are so rude."

"Well, right now you are pretending to be a human, so you should fit right in," Irene snaps.

Beda is now wearing clothes we gave her and a pair of dark glasses to hide her potential eye color shifts. Even my hair is tucked under a cap. People may recognize me. Most of Primaro saw my broadcast, and if they didn't watch the feed live, they've probably seen a recording. So, I'm keeping my head down as much as possible. The walk isn't too far. Hopefully, people are too wrapped up in their own business to notice me or Beda. So far, so good.

My chest tightens when a few gray patrol ships fly overhead and then out of sight. High on the building to my right, an Agrobot tends to the vines growing up the side as if this day is like any other.

Irene tracked down Dr. Owens apartment but couldn't get hold of him. After the explosion, apparently Dad's entire team was disbanded. So, we're headed to his last known address.

Another group of rowdy people passes us, but this time we keep our distance and walk closer to the building to stay out of their way.

"Where do you think they're all going?" I ask Max.

"I received updates from Hirata this morning, and there are a few rallies today for both sides. Since many of the city jobs are on hold for fear of possible attacks, people are free to let their minds wander. And it's getting some of them in trouble."

I think of the group of people Javen and I overheard before Max picked me up.

"Don't they remember Hammond was lying to us? I don't get why people are blindly following her plans. Why would anyone trust her?"

"Most of these people haven't even seen the Alku in person. Only a handful of Alku have come to the Arcadia side and shown themselves. The talks between them and the World Senate have been mostly closed-door. All these people know is that Earth is in trouble, the problem isn't getting solved, and they're not even allowed to talk about the issue. No one wants their family to die, and they don't know the Alku. What Hammond had to offer sounded pretty good to them. And although I don't agree with her solution, I can see why they're willing to go along with it."

Guilt stabs at me. Scaring people is partially my fault for making the announcement. Finding another way to stop the mining would have been better. But when Starfire harvesting began, it felt like there was no other way. The announcement had to be made or Hirata and Cooper never would have acted in support of the Alku.

"This is the one," Irene says while viewing a map on her Connect, interrupting my thoughts.

I gaze up at the grand building covered in foliage. In between the greenery, the building face is flecked with black and gold. I remember Dad showing me images of the apartment we were supposed to be assigned, and this looks a lot like the images of ours I saw online. Could be the very one.

We hustle through the open glass doors. I'm the last through right as a boom rumbles from the street— followed by an explosion. I turn to see if the fight is close.

But I see something else. *Someone* else.

Walking across the street is a short blond. Alina. My heart shudders. The last time we spoke, Hammond was searching for me. I dashed from my and Irene's dorm, accidentally leaving behind Dad's thumb drive with his video account of coming to Arcadia for the first time, which also included a portion of his plans for the Starfire. So, either she has the drive or Hammond does, if our dorm was searched.

Part of me wants to speak to Alina, but I have no idea if I can even trust her. And either the video is in the wrong hands, or it's not. There isn't much I can do about it now. I'll try to figure all the details out later. So, I turn to the others and let the glass doors slide shut behind me.

Beda is already inside the elevator. Max waves me over, and I sprint to him and smile. Inside, the floor is chosen, and the metal cab door shuts.

"He's on the sixth floor," Max says to Irene.

"And if he's not here, we're heading to the lab next?" Beda asks.

"Let's focus on one thing at a time," I answer.

I wouldn't mind taking Max to the lab, but I'm not sure I want Beda there, not yet anyway. I don't trust her enough.

The doors to the elevator open on our chosen floor, and we head straight toward Owens's apartment.

"Why don't you all step back?" I say, looking at the surveillance camera above the door. The viewing range is typically limited to the area right in front of the door and a little to the sides. "If he just sees me, he might be more likely to open up."

The rest of the group steps to the side, and I knock on the door and wait for footsteps or any other indication that he might be inside.

Nothing.

I wait for a moment before trying again. But still no sounds reach me from inside. I sigh, and my heart sinks into my stomach. Maybe he's not even living here now. If he wanted to fall off the map, it wouldn't surprise me. I turn toward the others.

"And you tried to contact him?" I ask Irene.

"Of course. That's the first step I took," she answers. "But no one has seen him."

I sigh and my shoulders slump.

Beda gives me a sour expression.

"What?" I ask her.

"Why are you just giving up so easily? Transport inside and see what you find."

I glance between Irene and Max. The last time I broke into a building, Javen and I were nearly killed. I don't want a repeat of that night.

"She's right," Max says. "There might be information we can use. Why waste the opportunity?"

My spine tenses at the thought of using the Intersection Starfire's power. But I hover my fingers over the face of the door and close my eyes. Slowly, I reach my hand to the collar of my shirt and touch the gem on the chain. As I visualize the opposite side of the door, the space around me compresses my body, and I gasp while opening my eyelids.

I did it. My hands touch the door's surface from inside the apartment, mirroring my actions from the opposite side before transporting. The room is mostly dark, but I can make out a few shapes of furniture. Only a tiny shred of light streams through a crack in a window shade. I reach toward the nearest wall to activate the lights.

"Hold it right there," a deep voice growls from behind me. "I have a gun."

My stomach flops.

"Dr. Owens, is that you?" I slowly rotate toward the voice.

"Who wants to know?"

"Cassiopeia Foster."

"Cassi? Richard's daughter?" The voice softens. "How did you get in here?"

I face him with my hands raised. I make out the silhouette of his bald head and body coming around the corner. His fist lowers, holding what does appear to be a gun.

I search my mind for an answer to his question, but all of them take too long to explain. "I need information, and I think you have what I need." I activate the lights from the panel by the door.

The man standing in front of me is older than my father. The skin around his eyes is heavily crinkled, and the overhead light reflects off his bald head. His brown trousers are rumpled, a style that coordinates with his stained white shirt. Under his eyes are dark circles, which give away his stress and lack of sleep. He stares at me for a moment and then his shoulders slump.

"I'm very sorry, Cassi. But I don't have any information for you." Dr. Owens turns from me. "I apologize that you came out among all the chaos and wasted your time. It's not safe on the streets today and you should return home as soon as you can."

I knit my brows at him. "You're lying. Why? I *know* you have information."

"My dear. I've been completely removed from your father's team. When the explosion happened, everything was disbanded."

"But Hirata has been elected. Surely you have the option to return to the project. I'm positive she wouldn't object."

Noises sound from the hall, and Owens lifts his weapon again.

"Those are just my friends," I say. "Can I let them in so they're not standing out in the hall?"

Owens lowers the gun again and steps forward to push me aside. "You really shouldn't have come here."

He reaches for the door handle. "I need to ask you to leave."

Well, I'm not going to. "I saw you last night at the lab."

Owens recoils. "What lab?"

"*Dad's lab.* I watched you go through the entrance last night."

A confused, pinched expression washes over his face for a moment, and then his nostrils flare with a sigh.

"Let your friends in."

I crack the door and find Beda, Max, and Irene waiting.

"You're okay?" Max asks.

"I'm fine," I say. "Come in."

"Something is happening on the street," Max says. "I just got a message. If you're fine, I think Beda and I will check it out."

I look to Dr. Owens and nod to Max. He knows I don't want Beda here. "We'll only be a few minutes. Make sure to stay close."

"Anything to get out of this building," Beda mutters and turns.

"I'll stay with Cassi," Irene says.

Max offers me a tentative smile. "Message us if there are any issues."

Irene steps into the apartment and gazes at Owens but doesn't say a word.

"Can we please ask you a few questions?" I say to him. "It's important."

He gestures us into the living room. I follow him and Irene and I sit on the couch. Dr. Owens stands, hands stuffed in his pockets. I don't know if I want to tell him that Dad is alive and that I got the directions from him. I'm pretty sure I can trust Dr. Owens, but he's not exactly forthcoming, and I'm not sure sharing the information is necessary at this time, anyway. Still, I press forward. I need to say something, and Irene is giving me a pointed look that says to start already. So, I do.

"Last night, Irene and I followed coordinates I . . . found when I came across a portion of Dad's back-up data. Both Irene and I watched you use the hand scanner, and you went inside the lab."

Owens raises an eyebrow, not speaking.

I'm going to need to give him more information to get him to trust me. "Irene and I were inside when you arrived."

He pinches his brows together. "Then there's no way you could have left unnoticed. The rear door is completely inaccessible."

"I got us out the same way I got into here. I transported."

"Like the Alku?" he asks with sudden interest.

"Inside, we downloaded files on Dad's Renewal project," I say, ignoring his question. "We know he had theorized the existence of the Intersection. How he believed the Starfire's source of energy there was much stronger than individually on each side."

Owens sighs. "The theory is what I'm continuing to work on at the lab. Well, attempting to work on. Without the team, I'm having a difficult time. The Board and Senate are unaware of the lab's existence, since your father hadn't presented the location to them yet. And he made sure the builders were sworn to secrecy and sent back to Earth several months before our arrival. I spend most of my time out there, trying to stay off the political radar. I only come here every few days and was hoping this would be one of my last times. Hirata may be in power now, but the situation could change very quickly."

"How close are you to completing the Renewal Project?" Irene asks.

"I needed Dr. Foster to consult with," he says. "There's a missing component I can't figure out yet. But I'm close."

"What if we came with you?" I ask and glance at Irene. She shrugs.

"Irene is a data genius, and I know my way around the Earthscape program. Plus, we have an Alku with us. She could be useful."

"An Alku?" he asks.

"The other girl in our group is Alku . . . the one who went down to the street." Irene says.

"We could meet at the lab tonight," I say.

Owens remains silent, considering what I've asked. "If you can get out there without detection, I'll agree. But first, I have something for you."

I give him a quizzical look as he turns and heads into one of his bedrooms. He returns clutching what appears to be a leather-bound book.

"Your father liked to keep a few of his items low-tech." He chuckles, but then his face turns serious. "After the explosion, most everything in our lab on the *Pathfinder* was confiscated, but I was able to get out with a few items and hide them. This journal was one of the items."

He holds the brown journal out to me, and I take it. On the outside is a thick strap encircling the whole book and a silver lock with an opening for some sort of strange key.

"Have you looked in it?" I ask.

"No. I didn't have a key, and I knew it was a personal item. Reading his journal just felt wrong."

I graze my fingers over the brown leather and then tuck the journal into my messenger bag. "Thanks. So, we'll see you tonight?"

"After 9 p.m."

Irene and I rise and head for the door when both of our Connects vibrate. I have just enough time to turn over my wrist and see the message from Max.

Get out.

A blast shudders the building, nearly knocking us off our feet.

"I knew this was coming," Dr. Owens says flatly. "I should have stayed out of the city."

I grab Irene and yank her back beside Owens. "I'll get us out of here," I say, clutching both their arms.

Despite not wanting to use the Starfire, I close my eyes and focus on the energy of the crystal that's dangling from my neck. The space around us warbles and then slams me back. I try again, and the same process repeats.

"It's not working this time!" Irene yells.

My heart pounds in my ears. Something is blocking me from transporting.

And then I see another problem. The wafting smoke coming in under Dr. Owens's door.

Chapter 13

"There's fire in the building. And smoke is already coming in under the door," I say to Max's holographic face now hovering over my Connect. "For some reason I can't transport, so have Beda come get us."

Smoke wafts into the room and I cough. Dr. Owens has disappeared into his bedroom again, and Irene is frantic in the kitchen, trying to find cloths to wet and place over our mouths.

"The northeast side of the building is engulfed." The hologram goes silent for a moment when he turns his head away to speak with someone. He turns back to me and shakes his head. "Beda can't transport you either. It's crazy out here. We made it across the street, but a group of guards is blocking the entrance to the building.

A handful of people from the Earth First rally are throwing hand bombs. Ships are flying in left and right."

A loud boom sounds, rattling the building again, and I wince.

"Another huge chunk on the side of your building is gone!"

"We need to figure out another way," I say, voice shaking. "If you need to, take Beda and get back to base."

"I'm not leaving you," Max says.

"There might be no choice! We shouldn't all die." My mind reels as I click off my Connect and Max's face vanishes.

Someone or something is blocking the Starfire's energy, keeping Beda and me from transporting.

"Dr. Owens!" Irene calls, as she finally holds up a couple of wet cloths. "We need to go."

"I'm coming!" he yells from the other room, his voice peppered with frustration.

After testing for heat, I throw open the still-cool door, but thick smoke wafts into the room.

"Let's go now, or there's a chance we're not getting out of here alive!" I yell to him.

I cover my mouth and nose with a cloth and then check for my gun tucked in the back of my pants. Still there.

Owens finally appears with a bag slung over his shoulder. "If this is as bad as I think, I'm probably not coming back here," he says, his face glistening with sweat. "I need this for my research."

I recheck my bag for Dad's journal before tossing Dr. Owens a cloth.

"You get everything?" I ask him.

"I doubt it," he says. "But the situation is what it is."

The three of us dash from the apartment as two other people from this floor push past, nearly knocking me to the ground. I throw my palm to the wall to catch myself. Orange flames lick at the opposite end of the hall. The smoke stings my eyes, and I hustle to locate an exit other than the elevator.

I refuse to die today.

The man and woman ahead of us throw open a door leading to the staircase. Typically, when there's a fire, the building's bot crew is released with chemical fire retardant and the building's water system is activated. But there's nothing. Not even alarms. The building is burning to the ground, and the residents inside could be trapped. Could this whole event have been planned? My lungs burn as we dart into the stairwell and thunder down the steps. Finally, our feet hit the street level and we charge out of the building and into pandemonium. A group of people across the way hold laser pistols and are shooting at a group of soldiers who are running down the street. Overhead, two small ships hover in the sky.

With a sharp inhale, I take in a lungful of somewhat breathable air. Then I stuff the corner of my wet cloth into my pocket, in case of more smoke. Quickly, I scan the area and watch as a guy throws something into a building on the next block. Fire explodes from the opening and sends debris flying. A mix of terror and anger fills the faces on the street as some people scatter while others try to prevent them from fleeing. I scan the crowds for Max and Beda, but I can't see anyone familiar.

"Where are the others?" I shout over the noise to Irene. She remains next to Dr. Owens, helping him carry his bag from the building. I tap my Connect, but nothing happens. That's not working either now? What's going on?

"Come back with us," I call to Owens. "Then we can figure all this out."

Irene urges him forward in the direction we need to go. "Keep your heads down and don't make eye contact," Irene yells over the noise. "Don't stop until we're clear."

I readjust my bag and snatch the gun from my waistband. Irene does the same with hers, looking a million times more comfortable with her weapon.

"Be careful with that," she says into my ear. "It's easy to shoot the wrong person."

JENETTA PENNER

I nod and push my way into the crowd. Several times I check to see if Irene and Owens are still behind me and then re-orient myself. Still no Max and Beda.

Two blocks away, just as the crowd seems to be thinning, a militia of silver soldier bots rounds the corner of a building and cuts me off from Irene like a knife. I raise up on my toes and try to see what direction Irene and Owens are being pushed toward when an explosive detonates near them. The last thing I see is Dr. Owens being thrown to the ground before the bots completely block my view and force me away. I scream for Irene, but the soldier bots are a relentless swarm. Though I tried to avoid them, several nearly hit me and I slam to the sidewalk. I push to my feet again, keeping hold of my gun.

"Hey," a voice calls out to me.

I swing my head toward the sound and point the gun in the direction of the voice. Alina is coming straight for me, throwing her hands in the air when she spots my weapon.

I lower the gun. "I need to get Irene!" I scream.

"*We need* to get off the street!" she yells and grabs my arm, pulling me farther from where I last saw Irene.

Tears pour from my eyes. "I can't leave her!"

But Alina doesn't listen or stop until she gets us to a quieter alley between two buildings.

My chest heaves and I strain to catch my breath. "What's going on?"

"I don't know," she says, looking around. "I was on my way to a delivery, and one of those Earth First rallies erupted. Everyone went crazy. My Connect isn't working, so I couldn't get any news or figure out a safe way to escape. Then I spotted you."

I slump against the wall, and my bag drops off my arm, flipping the top open. The brown journal catches my eye. I close the flap, and Alina reaches out and helps me secure the strap to my shoulder. I check around the corner. Most of the people have scattered by now. But no sign of Irene or Dr. Owens. Or Max or Beda. I can't wander around here and search for them. My best bet is to head directly to our base.

"Do you have a safe place to go?" I ask.

Alina nods. "Yeah, a couple of blocks from here."

"You sure?" I've no idea if I should bring Alina with us, but I can't just leave her out here, either.

"I'll be fine. I'm expected, and I need to show up for my meeting or they'll think I'm dead," she says and adjusts her shirt. "Stay safe."

Alina squares herself and then dashes from the safety of our niche between the buildings.

I grip my gun and do the same.

Chapter 14

race toward the perimeter of the base but must push my way through a crowd held up and turned away by guards.

"I need to get in!" I yell.

The guard scans me up and down.

"I'm Richard Foster's daughter. This is where I'm supposed to be."

With a sudden wide-eyed look of recognition, he pulls me out of the crowd and pilots me to a check-in station.

"Palm ID?" a female guard asks.

I raise my hand and she scans my palm. The scanner beeps.

"Get inside," she says. "But I'm not sure how long we're going to be here."

With no time to ask questions, I sprint from the guard station to the building we're staying in. Overhead fly five—no six—ships defending our airspace from the other side's aircraft.

I bite my lip as I run. The tang of iron skims over my tongue. I wipe the taste from my mouth as I sprint by others who also are hurrying toward safety.

Another armed guard meets me at the building entrance, and I repeat the palm ID process. He, too, lets me pass.

I take the stairs down to the floor where Irene works and head toward the office she was last in. I throw open the partially cracked door and find all three of my friends inside—not that Beda is a friend, but I'm still glad she's here. Relief travels over my entire body. Beda has her back against the wall with her arms crossed over her chest. Irene is sitting at her station, head in hands and crying—not something I would expect from her. Max is pacing. My heart jitters. Max turns, sees me, and races my way, throwing his arms around me.

"You're okay," he says into my hair.

His embrace feels good, safe. "Yeah," I say, about to tell them how Alina pulled me away from the soldier bots, but then I notice not everyone is here. "Where's Dr. Owens?"

A somber expression washes over Max's face and he focuses on the floor.

"Apparently he was with Irene," Beda says flatly, "and he was shot."

Irene quietly sobs into her hands. I walk over and kneel in front of my friend.

"I'm sure there was *nothing* you could do," I say.

She glances up at me. "I could have. I saw the shooter raising his gun before he hit Owens. I should have shot him first. But I didn't . . . couldn't." She finishes the last word in a faint, choked whisper.

I slip my arms around her waist and lean my head on her lap. We all stay silent for several minutes as the pops of distant bombs rumble through the walls.

"I did get his bag," Irene finally whispers once more.

I look up at her. She tips her head to her left side. The bag lies on the floor, a red stain of blood marring the fabric. Maybe there's something inside that will be helpful to us. I scoot over to the bag and grab the strap just as my Connect vibrates on my wrist. The devices are working again.

An image appears on the screen.

Hammond.

My stomach tenses. I had hoped she was dead, though the chances of that were slim. And I'm sure she's behind all this.

"Greetings, Primaro." Hammond says, her features stiff and emotionless. She's dressed in a stark, black suit with her hair pulled from her face, accentuating the severe angles of her cheekbones.

The camera pans wide, and I recognize the outside of the Capitol building. Off camera, the crowd is yelling and screaming. I can't tell yet if it's in support or defiance of Hammond.

Hammond raises her hands in the air and the crowd quiets. I know that whatever is going to happen next can't be good. My mind races with possibilities, and the only plausible option right now is to travel to the Alku side. Hammond doesn't understand yet how to use the Starfire to transport to Paxon. At least going there might give us time to figure out a plan and keep us out of harm's way. But then, I remember how neither Beda nor I can transport. And if mining starts again, removing Starfire will likely destroy the Paxon side of the Intersection anyway.

I grit my teeth back to reality.

"We are humans, and Earth is our responsibility," Hammond says. "If there is a way to save the planet and the billions of people who still live there, we must move forward down *that* path."

Enzo Leon stands behind Hammond, along with several members of the World Senate whom I vaguely recognize. What are they planning to do? And what happened to the truce and Hirata's election? But if

Hammond has taken over the Capitol building, then all that hope is out the window.

The camera pans again, showing several faces I don't recognize, and then two I do from the files I saw. Dr. Ann Jonas and Dr. Grant Abbot, the two other former members of Dad's team. Their faces are stiff, expressions nervous. Jonas's ash-blond hair is more tousled than what I remember from the immaculate image on her ID. Like they're being forced to stand before the cameras. Probably the only reason Dr. Owens isn't up there is because he had been hiding at Dad's lab . . . before he died, that is.

"Earth has claimed Arcadia, and we *will* take the resources we need to save our primary home. During my absence, my scientists have been working on a way to harness the Starfire's power. Our first step was to counter the Alku's defenses that were blocking us from the city of Primaro and also preventing us from entering the Starfire fields. And we successfully achieved step one." She pauses a beat. "We now have a series of devices called Inhibitors."

The scene switches to show several small silver hovers, the same ones I saw over Owens's building during the attack. That's what must be keeping me from transporting. Do Javen or any of the others even know what's happening here?

I scan around the room. Irene is still seated and stares at her holographic computer screen, which displays Hammond too largely for my taste. My eyes are drawn to the President's neckline where the Starfire necklace she ripped from my neck now hangs. My stomach roils at the sight of my crystal.

Max has slipped partially out into the hall and speaks to someone out there. Beda paces on my left, teeth clenched and fingers pumping in and out of her fists.

"We have full control of the Turner Space Fold," Hammond continues, "and hundreds of miners are ready to begin harvesting the Starfire for Earth to begin the healing process."

How am I going to warn Javen and the Council, if they don't know? There must be a way to get word to them. But if I'm blocked from using the Starfire, I can't contact Javen.

"The city is on immediate lockdown," she says to the camera. "Any and all job placements will be reassessed. Our new focus in Arcadia will be Starfire extraction and the utilization of this resource. If we do not take this route, great portions of the Earth will succumb to the atmosphere's breakdown. Mining the Starfire is our best chance to ensure the survival of our species. To secure a future where humans survive and thrive, we must prevent anyone who blocks our way to save Earth. The Alku are an evil people. This evaluation of their species was determined when attempting to make a peaceful agreement between our kind and theirs. They refused."

Nausea wells inside me. I know the Alku are willing to help save Earth. My dad was developing a plan for restoration. It's Hammond who doesn't want to utilize this option.

The crowd erupts with chants of "Save Earth, Save Earth!"

The camera pans back again, and my eyes widen as I see three people led out in front of Hammond—Hirata, Cooper, and Luca Powell. Since Luca supported Hirata, he must now be Hammond's enemy. The three of them are secured with hands behind their backs.

"These three Board members have been charged with treason against Earth," Hammond says. "They attempted to make private deals with the Alku in order to save themselves."

Hirata's face is damp with tears as a guard shoves her forward. This can't be happening. Hirata was supposed to fix everything. The Senate was swinging to her side. They just elected her yesterday.

My fists clench in desperation. Once Wirrin's faction finds out what's happening, it will only lead to war. And if Hammond is aware of the Starfire's power within the Intersection, she will use it. I grit my teeth. Don't these people understand attempting to save Earth by stealing the Starfire could annihilate *all* of humanity?

I look around the room to find Max and ask if he knows anything about the announcement, but he's gone. I return my attention to the screen just as Hirata hits the ground. A guard stands next to her, laser pistol still extended. Wasting no time, the next guard shoves Cooper forward and the same is done to him. I retch, but nothing comes.

The two bodies lie limp on the ground as Luca is brought to the front. His usual swagger and bravado is replaced with terror as his legs shake beneath him. A guard raises his weapon, and Luca drops to his knees.

I choke on a forming sob. Despite my distaste for Luca Powell, I have no desire to see him executed.

"I'm loyal, I'm loyal!" he yells. "Please don't kill me!"

The guard glances at Hammond, and she raises her hand to pause the proceedings. She walks forward and kneels in front of Luca, and then leans in to whisper into his ear. Then Hammond rises and returns focus onto the camera and hushed crowd.

A tense grin stretches across her lips and she extends her hand to Luca. He takes it, and she pulls him to his feet.

"We are generous and desire to forgive. Luca Powell has extended his loyalty to the will of the World Senate."

Luca darts his eyes over the crowd and then looks to the ground.

"The Senate *will* display mercy. But traitors must be eliminated."

As the words exit Hammond's mouth, the building we're in shudders with an explosion. The holograms snap off from our Connects and the computer screen.

Max throws open the door. "Hammond staged a coup. At least twenty of the World Senate members have been assassinated and many are missing. We're evacuating the building."

"Where are we going to go?" asks Irene. "It's probably too late!"

Beda slams her fist on the wall. "Why did I have to be *here*?!"

Irene grabs Dr. Owens's bag. She stands and straightens out her shirt, then drops her shoulders from their tense position. "I'm getting our stuff from below." She looks to Max. "I have time, right?"

Max hits his Connect and studies the screen for a second. "Be back in ten minutes."

Irene nods. "I'll get your things, too, Cassi."

I don't even get a chance to answer before she's out the door.

"We're going to that lab of yours," Beda demands.

"We can't go there. Hammond's people will find us and then Dad's data."

"They may locate the lab eventually anyway," Beda says. "We need to get out there, find everything your father was working on, and destroy the lot. Burn it all to the ground. Otherwise, Hammond could use the information against us."

"Destroy it? No way!" I say while thinking of the AI version of my mother. It's weird and all, but seeing her again brought me a measure of comfort. "You just don't want any humans mastering the Starfire. We need to get out there and access all the information. Once the data is secured, *then* we can wipe it out."

A blaring alarm sounds through the building and I clap my hands over my ears.

"Please calmly proceed to the exits," an unseen male voice says. "Escorts will be waiting to evacuate all personnel from the premises."

"Where are they taking us?" I swing to Max.

"Some place safe?" Max says.

"And where would that be?" I ask. "There probably isn't a safe place in the city."

"Hence why we're going to the lab," Beda growls.

Max studies me and I nod. But before he has the chance to move, Irene steps through the door with bags slung over her shoulder. She shrugs mine off and tosses it to me. "I got hold of Trav. He can get us an all-terrain vehicle. It's waiting below." Irene pivots her attention to Beda. "Unless you and Cassi can transport the four of us?"

"The Starfire still isn't working or I would have returned to Paxon already," Beda says.

"We'll need data storage," I say, ignoring Beda.

"Already packed." Irene pats her bag.

"Then let's go," I say, suppressing my fear. I need to keep a straight head on my shoulders right now.

Chapter 15

We sprint down the stairs, against the stream of people who are making their way out of the building. I'm not sure whether the people in the crowd or our group feels more like salmon swimming against the current toward our impending deaths. Probably all of us.

We hit the underground parking lot, and Trav races our direction.

"You should have just left the vehicle for us and got out of here, Trav," Irene says.

He tips his head. "Does that mean you care, Irene?"

"Give it a rest, Trav," she says. "I don't want *anyone* to die here."

"I wanted to make sure no one else claimed the Rover." Despite visibly tense shoulders, he smiles at Irene and then runs around a corner. A few seconds later, he appears again with a small, enclosed off-road vehicle with four seats.

"It's pretty cozy in there," Trav says as he swings the driver's side door up to reveal both the front and rear seats.

Beda gives the vehicle a scowl, and I'm guessing she's never ridden in such a thing. And being in such close quarters with three humans probably seems unbearable, too.

Max places a hand on the driver's seat door, but Irene cuts him off. "No way, buddy. I'm driving."

He throws his hands to chest height in surrender and then races to the passenger side. Beda slides in the front seat before he can get in, so he takes the back next to me.

"You all be careful out there," Trav says as he begins pushing down the driver's side hatch.

"Take care of yourself," Irene says before the door snaps shut.

Beda pulls down the other side. Within seconds, Irene swings us around and we're rolling out through the rising gate while the vehicle's console lights up with data.

"I'm uploading a program to block others from tracking us," Irene says.

Beda growls, "Just get us out of the city."

Irene glares at her. "That's what we're doing. If you have something helpful to add, we welcome your opinion. Otherwise, be quiet."

Beda glares out the front window.

Irene taps in the last of the instructions, and I follow Beda's gaze. To our left, a group of armed soldiers run toward an escape hover. The same vessel that people from our building, as well as others, have lined up to board. A single enemy fighter ship sweeps across the sky on a direct route toward the craft.

"The incoming ship is aiming for the escaping people." The words barely escape as my heart jumps to my throat.

Irene manually takes a sharp turn, momentarily disengaging the autodrive, throwing me into Max. He helps me up just in time to see laser shots fire from the ground. The blast clocks the edge of the single fighter and sends it off course and out of sight. Then a plume of smoke billows into the air. From behind us, people speed up their loading process, and I watch until Irene tears around a building and the waiting crowd is out of sight.

"Where are they taking them?" I ask.

"Outside of the city," Max says. "The ship has camouflage ability, and if they can escape, the tech will keep everyone safe for a while."

"How long?" Irene asks.

"Not sure," he says. "Arcadia is a big place, but Hammond wants to make examples of traitors. One of the pilots is in encrypted contact with me. So, we can stay in the loop."

The vehicle accelerates once the forest comes into view. From the side window, I spot two ships overhead. But they pass us, probably ordered to focus on the larger buildings and vessels rather than small off-road vehicles.

Under the cover of trees, I let out a breath and touch Max's hand on the seat beside me. I smile, give his fingers a squeeze and then release, pulling my hand back onto my lap. There's a huge part of me that does regret kissing him, no matter what I said. Our kiss complicates things, and everything is already so complicated. I need to think of something else and decide to lean toward Beda.

"What if we could transport everyone onto the Alku side once they are out of the city? Maybe it will work?"

She twists her head toward me. "May I speak now?"

I sigh. "Yes, I want your opinion."

She squints her brown eyes at me, and her face takes on a pinched expression. "No," she says flatly.

"Why not?" I ask. "It will give us more time."

"Even if we could, there are too many. Taking more than a few across is dangerous for our bodies. And it would also put the Alku in more danger, by harboring humans. My people will sense the humans' presence. And *that* will cause even more dissension."

"What if Vihann agrees?"

"My father's camp will not, even if Vihann and the Council say yes," she says. "The Luminary's stance is to save the Alku people. He only allowed the Starfire's use to defend humans. But the situation has changed. Now your people will attempt to use the Starfire as a weapon for themselves. My people's goal is now to stop Starfire weapons from forming. Helping humans, even ones who are not immediately dangerous, will not be high on his priorities."

I want to argue, but truthfully, I don't blame her. Humans have done nothing but take from the Alku, and it's only going to get worse.

The rest of the trip is spent in near silence. Beda slumps in the front and Irene keeps her attention on the controls, occasionally checking out the windows for overhead ships. Max stays engrossed in his Connect to relay the few tidbits of intel coming through on the escape ships. My stomach churns, and I fidget with my fingers still resting on my lap.

"We're nearly there," Irene finally says, breaking the silence. "I'm going to park us a little way off so we can scope out the area first to see if the lab is safe."

She pulls us under a thick canopy of trees and we exit the vehicle. As my feet press to the ground, the Starfire on my neck vibrates against my skin, and I pull the necklace out of my collar. In my fingers, the gem glows.

"It's active here," I say.

Beda twists to see what I'm talking about, and her eyes grow wide. "Meaning whatever Hammond is using to block transportation only has a limited range." She tenses her jaw. "I'm heading back to my father. My people must know what's going on."

I open my mouth to tell her she should wait until we get all the data from Dad's lab. But I'm not fast enough, and she vanishes. Gone to Paxon, I'm sure.

I tuck the Starfire inside my shirt and secure my bags to my shoulder as the other two survey the area for ships or troops. But from what I can tell, there's no other activity besides us.

"Seems clear to me," Max says.

I agree and wave the two of them toward the lab. This time, since I know the structure is there, I can make out the building's outline despite the camouflage. After a short walk to the front, I place my hand on the scanner and the door slides away.

"Welcome, Cassiopeia Foster," my mom's disembodied AI voice says, but I ignore it.

"I'll go to the lab and start working on the files," Irene says. "After you get me into the system, why don't the two of you check the rest of the place out? See if there's anything else we can use here?" Sadness shadows her eyes. "Dr. Owens did say he was living here; maybe you can find his quarters."

We head into the lab, and when we enter, my mother appears again. "How may I help—"

"Disengage visual AI," I say, and the virtual version of Mom disappears. I inhale deeply and suppress the emotions attempting to well up. Max touches my back, and calm instantly settles over my body. I log Irene onto the system after I drop my bags in the corner.

"Work as fast as you can," I say. "We have no idea how long we're going to be safe here or whether anyone else knows about this place."

Irene removes her upgraded DataPort from her bag, as well as a few other familiar pieces of equipment. "Leave it up to me," she says. "This is what I do."

I turn and head from the room. Max follows.

"Your mother was so beautiful," Max says. "I had seen her once, but never so close."

"I think this version of her is programmed to the age she was when my parents got married."

"She would be proud of you, you know," Max says.

The comment stings. "I'm a complete mess, Max. What are you talking about?"

An activated door slides back, revealing small sleeping quarters. The bed is left unmade, and to the side is a small desk.

Max touches my arm, stopping me.

"Your mother was incredibly brave. She was willing to put aside how so many people were telling her and your father that colonization within fifty years was impossible. She helped make Arcadia happen anyway. Against all the odds, you found your father, and you're still working to save the Alku. You are very much like her. I'm pretty sure she would see those qualities in you."

I choke away my emotion and touch Mom's ring on my finger. Even though I want to fall to the floor and curl up in a ball, I straighten my shoulders and offer Max a soft smile of thanks. Then, I head directly to the desk and begin searching the drawers. I locate nothing but a few personal items, however. Nothing of value. Taking my lead, Max checks the closet and shrugs.

He and I search the two other rooms in the building as well as the kitchen.

"I don't think Dad planned for the building to be fully functional until he returned to Arcadia."

"Makes sense," Max says as we enter the lab, where we find Irene working furiously in front of the holographic screen.

"Any news from your friend?" I look at Max, but he shakes his head. I'm not sure if no news is a good or bad thing.

"All I know are their destination coordinates," he says.

"Well, I guess the directions will help us locate them later." I sit at the station next to Irene and bring up the Earthscape program. "What are the coordinates?"

Max pairs his Connect with the computer and sends the information. Within a blink, a three-dimensional map appears in front of me. The program shows the hover's route and the approximate distance to the destination point, based on the last data sent to Max's Connect. The escape destination is located along the base of the Tahm Range, where there appears to be a cave system. If they can arrive in time, the caves should be a decent place to hide. But those larger hovers are not designed for speed.

"How are you coming along on the downloads?" I ask Irene.

"Getting there," she says, "but there's so much, I'm not entirely sure what's most important."

"Just get everything you can," I say.

"There are several more encrypted files that I've run across. Want me to take a chance and download all the data?"

"Yea—" I start to say.

"Warning," Mom's AI voice interrupts. "An unknown external device is attempting to access my computer system."

"What's that mean?" I ask Irene.

"It means another hacker is attempting to get into the lab's computer system."

Nerves ignite and tingle in my chest. Someone knows about the lab. "Can you block them?"

"What do you think I'm doing?" Irene growls. "We need to get everything possible downloaded and purge the system. Otherwise, Hammond is going to have access to all the data Dr. Foster must have been hiding."

"Five incoming craft within a one-mile radius," the AI says.

"There's no way for us to get everything!" Irene says. "Time is running out."

"Then you'll need to purge the data now," Max demands.

"If we do that, Hammond has won."

I stare at the holo-screen in front of me, which now shows an overhead view of Arcadia. My mind shifts as if I'm flying above the jungle, watching the land below. In my state, I feel the Starfire pulse on my neck, and the energy ripples through me. We can't do this without my dad. He's the only human who understands the Starfire so completely. He also knows how to save the Alku and probably Earth.

My consciousness is caught somewhere between the lab and another place entirely. I can hear Irene calling my name and then my mom's AI voice relaying that the ships are now in our immediate vicinity. But none of this bothers me as warmth from the Starfire travels the length of my body.

I begin to relax right as a sharp sensation hits me. It's as if I slam into a block of ice, and a bright cyan light blinds me. I let out a scream but no sound escapes.

"What did you do, Cassi?" a muffled voice asks. I don't know whose.

But then my mom's voice cuts through, and the ghost of her hand strokes my forehead.

"Incoming ships have vanished," she says. "Danger averted."

Chapter 16

A chill shudders through my body, and my breath hitches. "What happened?" I say as I shoot up into a seated position. My head spins, and every part of my body aches.

"I don't know yet." Instead of Mom, Irene kneels beside me.

"Are the ships still coming?" I feel as if I might throw up at any second.

Irene tilts her head. "Not according to the AI."

"Where'd they go?"

Max jogs into the lab, pale. "I don't think they went anywhere. *We* did."

The Starfire pulses against my leg, and I reach into my pocket to pull the other gem out. Just holding the crystal tight in my fist returns a trickle of strength to my body. "Did I transport us? Why are we still in the lab?"

"Apparently you moved the *entire* building," he says.

"What?" Irene scans the room.

"I checked, and the outside isn't the same. First off, it's night, and second, everything has this creepy blue color."

My stomach twists at Max's words, and I try to stand but fall to the ground. "Are we in the Intersection?"

"How am I supposed to know?" he says. "But we're not in the same place as before. The Rover is gone." He considers me for a second and then softens his voice. "Are you okay?"

I lay my head on the floor and clutch the Starfire. Waves of calm roll through me. "I think I will be in a moment."

I close my eyelids and allow the energy to radiate to each limb. To heal me. Just like the energy healed Javen from the laser gun wound after he transported us to his side of the Intersection the first time. Thoughts of Javen consume my every thought. The pain of not having him with me shoots through my body, and I curl into a ball. Instinctively, I summon for him. But nothing happens.

Despite my disappointment, my strength continues to return slowly, and I open my eyes. Both of my friends look concerned. Max reaches to help me up, but I avoid his touch, not quite sure where to place my feelings for him alongside the ones I have for Javen.

"I'm okay," I say and push myself up. "Show me the outside." I avoid Max and focus on Irene.

"Follow me," he says.

I can sense Max's confusion, but I still don't look at him as I make my way down the hall and through the lab's front door. Once outside, my gaze snaps upward to the aurora-filled sky, similar to the Alku side but more intense. We are on a hill of sorts, I realize. Above us, gasses brush across the night sky and over the moons in bright blue-green.

"We *are* in the Intersection." I scan the landscape and recognize the area. At the bottom of the hill, I spot the cave my dad was living in. "That's where my dad is."

"Do you think he can help us?" Irene asks.

A stone churns in my stomach.

"Maybe he can," I say. "His lab is here now, and he can better make sense of all the data anyway."

"Then we should get him," Max says.

We? I grit my teeth together. I have no idea of Dad's current state. "Let me go see. You two wait here, and I'll bring him."

Irene sighs but agrees, as does Max. Though, by the tense expression on his face, I can tell he senses my distance.

"I won't be long." I trudge along the same course I used the first time I was here to find Dad. Again, I follow the path to the cave opening and walk through. Inside, light flickers on the cavern walls, as before, and then I round the corner that previously led me to him.

"Dad," I call out when I don't see him.

The space appears much the same as before, with no additional items he's brought to this side.

"Dad?" I call out again, this time louder.

"Cassi?" Dad emerges from around a corner I hadn't noticed in my previous visits. The cave must extend farther than I thought.

Dad smiles widely and the corners of his eyes crinkle. He looks normal again. My heart melts as this is the man I've always known.

"Daddy!"

I run to him, my arms open wide, and he pulls me into a strong embrace. I squeeze him and let loose.

"Did you bring an Alku with you?" He glances around.

I knit my brows together. Dad asked me the same question the last time, and I had a strange feeling then as I do now. But I smile and push the reaction away. "No, but I might have brought something better. Your lab?"

Dad stills. I'm not even sure he's breathing. "You brought *my lab*?"

I fill him in on all the details from today: Hirata and Cooper's executions; how Hammond took over and swayed the World Senate; about Dr. Abbot and Dr. Jonas from his team, who are now working for Hammond; and

I tell him about the Alku supporters who are on their way out of the city and plan to hide at the Tahm Range.

"Jonas and Abbot would never work for Hammond unless they were forced to." Dad pinches the bridge of his nose. "How did we get here? I should have been on Arcadia to convince the Senate."

"You would probably really be dead. At least with your lab here, you can continue your work."

"What about Matt Owens? You didn't mention him. I need his assistance."

"We might have some of his data . . . but he didn't make it."

Dad's expression crumbles in disappointment.

"Do you think you could complete the experiment with the portal device at the lab—if you had all of Owens's data?"

Dad nods. "Possibly. But tell me again, how did you bring my entire lab here?"

I pull the Starfire he gave me from my shirt and present it to him. "I used this."

"One crystal was able to do *that*?"

Not wanting to waste time, I pilot Dad up toward the hill and the lab's entrance, which is wide open.

"This is amazing, Cassi. Your ability is beyond what I know even the Alku can do with the Starfire. I've been able to bring a few small items to me and send the apples across to the Alku side, but that's it. Bringing a whole building inside the Intersection is something else entirely."

"It must be because my Starfire is from the Intersection."

Dad stops me and places his hands on my shoulders. "There's a possibility the answer might be *you*."

I furrow my eyebrows, confused. Could my connection to Javen be doing this?

Before I can ask any more questions, Dad squeezes my shoulders and his eyes grow distant. "I have an idea for the Hirata supporters."

He hurries toward the lab's opening.

"Welcome, Cassiopeia and Richard Foster," my mother's voice sounds.

Dad stops and stares at the walls as recognition hits him. The distracted look he had a moment ago falls away.

"Why did I ever make that AI?" he asks.

I offer him a sad shrug.

"The whole thing was a joke for your mom. She had teased me occasionally about how the lab was my girlfriend, so I had a friend program the AI to be her. I guess I had forgotten to disable the program."

"Why didn't Dr. Owens turn it off?"

Dad lifts a single shoulder in a slight shrug, like the one I had given him. "The program is fairly complex. He probably didn't want to destroy any of the AI's functionality." He presses his lips together and then curses under his breath. "Why did Owens have to die, too? I need him here." Pain flashes in his gaze again, and then he briefly closes his lids, as if in thought. He takes a settling breath and focuses on me once more. "I think I know enough, and with your ability to channel the Starfire, I believe we can make it work."

"Make what work?" I ask.

"Open a portal with only a small amount of Starfire energy and then move all the refugees into the Intersection."

He turns in the hallway and steps toward the lab, but I grab his arm. "What if Hammond finds out about this place? Who knows what she might do with the Starfire from here?"

"Cassi, this is an emergency situation. Hammond will find those people, if they're even still alive. I know her—she's relentless."

A shiver runs up my spine, and I know what Dad says is true. The caves will mean a day, maybe two, of safety. If Dad's former team members are still on his side but are being forced to work for Hammond, they may try to throw her off the refugees' scent for a short period of time. But his former team members can only hold out for so long before she realizes what they're doing. They know everything about this planet, I'm sure, including the best places within range of Primaro for a large group of people to hide. And Hammond is well aware of their knowledge.

I study Dad, my eyes narrowing slightly. He seems mostly okay now. He was far different when I was here before. Maybe his body needed time to adjust to the Starfire. An urge to speak with Javen pulses hot through me. But time is short.

"Okay," I say. "But only until we can figure out a better alternative. The Alku won't even have to know that we're bringing more Earthlings into the Intersection."

Dad nods and guides me to the lab.

Inside, Max and Irene have a holographic screen activated, scrolling over data in the Earthscape program.

They both crane their necks our way and their tense jaws soften with relief.

"Dr. Foster," Max says and stands.

"This is Irene and Max," I say. "They both helped me through everything after the explosion."

"You transported people *and* a building? Simultaneously?"

I nibble the inside of my lip, embarrassed. "Yeah, I did."

Pride radiates from Dad's smile and I swallow back my nerves. Then he turns and extends his hand to Max, who takes it, looking a bit starstruck.

"I appreciate you befriending Cassi," Dad says to both of them.

"It hasn't been easy," Irene jokes, dissolving some of the seriousness in the room.

"I'll bet," Dad quips in reply. "Now what have we got here?" He looks at the display.

"This is the last known location of the refugees," Max says. "My Connect went out when we crossed into the Intersection, so I'm trying to figure out why this other stuff all works in here."

"Likely because everything is powered by Starfire energy," Dad says. "When I came to Arcadia the first time and became aware of the Starfire, I had my team start working on figuring out how the crystal's energy functioned. This lab was designed as a test facility. I saw how the Alku lived and wanted to integrate the ideas into human design and function." Dad looks to me. "It was important to your mother." Dad stares off as if he's remembering something for a moment and then scratches his head. "May I have a seat?"

Irene stands and offers Dad her chair.

"Show me Project Renewal."

"Verifying voice authorization," the AI says. "Approved."

Files fly onto the display and Dad studies them. He taps a few while swiping away others he doesn't want.

"I'm accessing the lab's power source, which is a combination of Starfire from each side of the Intersection. I found that using the two together was more efficient, and now I know why. They were partially mimicking the Starfire's power inside the Intersection. Owens set everything up before he died." He looks to me. "You said you have the destination coordinates of the refugees?"

"Everything is entered into the Earthscape program," Irene says. "It gave their estimated location based on the last time Max was in contact with them."

"Well, that will have to do," Dad says and pairs the two programs together. "Nothing of this magnitude has been tested, but this should create a portal around our current location. Problem is, I have no idea how long the portal will remain open."

"Maybe I can help with that," I say, pulling the Starfire from under my shirt. The gem glows and pulses in my hand.

"Your help is what I'm counting on," Dad says. "If you were able to pull the lab across the dimensions, I'm going to need you to visualize and yank in the vessels holding the refugees."

"But this has never been tested," Max says, his voice thick which concern. "It could totally backfire and hurt Cassi."

I look to Dad, but he's staring at the display. I'm pretty sure neither Max nor Irene sees, but for a brief second, cyan swirls in Dad's eyes. The sight of it sends a shock into my stomach and firmly reminds me: the longer we are in the Intersection, the more we are likely to be affected . . . good or bad.

But right now, the Intersection is our only option. The Starfire's power, too.

"We have to try," I say.

"That's my girl." Dad looks to me, his eyes now normal.

"Are you sure?" Max asks. "You don't have to do this."

"I'm sure," I say.

"What can I do?" Irene asks.

"Can you keep this program running?" Dad asks and stands.

"No problem." Irene takes his seat, studies the display and immediately gets to work.

Dad claps Max on the shoulder and leads him to the door. He gestures for me to follow. "The energy field should be building outside. My estimate? It'll take no more than a minute or two to reach the right spot. Once the portal opens, I need you to reach your contact. Hopefully, they're close and can get within range. The opening should allow the communication to get through."

Outside, I'm immediately hit with a thick wave of energy. It's as if we're swimming through water. This is a sensation I've felt before, when Javen used the Starfire to cloak us from vision. The space around the lab emits a slight, pulsing cyan glow that intensifies by the second. My heart races as I feel the energy moving through my body. Instinctively, I close my eyes and let everything fall away.

"Are you ready, Cassi?" I hear my dad's muffled voice say, but I'm already gone.

I find myself standing in sunshine instead of darkness. The Tahm Range is still in the distance, but we must be miles away from Primaro. I spin, expecting Dad and Max to be here, but they're not. Sudden fear shudders through me. What if it's not working correctly? What if Max couldn't contact the pilot?

I watch a formation of ten ships zoom past above me. My eyes widen as panic sets in. I look again in the direction they're heading and now I see them . . . three large carrier ships full of refugees.

A shot fires from an enemy ship and hits the lead carrier. I suck in a sharp breath as the vessel bursts into flames and pitches downward.

I unhook my necklace and clutch the Starfire, anger burning inside me, and focus on the three ships. As I do, a cyan burst pours from my body and I focus the energy straight at the escapees, yanking the trio of hovers across a dimension and into the Intersection.

Chapter 17

pull back into the Intersection just as the third ship crashes into the ground and explodes with a massive roar. A plume of cyan fire and gray smoke grapple for the night sky.

In a panic I whip around and scream for Max and my dad, but there's not much we can do. Turning back, I see the two other ships pull to a stop, and within seconds, people scramble out of the open hatches.

Lightheadedness overwhelms me and my knees buckle. My limp body falls to the ground in a heap. Every part of me ripples with searing pain, but my eyes remain wide, taking in the horror.

Dad and Max run to my side, and everything blurs.

"You got her?" Max asks in a muffled voice.

"See how you can help at the ships," Dad tells Max, but his voice is distant, too.

My eyelids blink open and shut as I fight to stay conscious.

"What's going on?" I hear Irene but can't see her.

"Go help, Max," Dad says. "Cassi . . . Cassi." He grabs for my hand and pushes an object into it.

The second he does, my vision fills with brilliant cyan and I gasp, sitting up. I peer down to see that I'm holding my glowing Starfire. Tingling flows from the crystal into my skin, and currents of my energy return.

"Go help them," I say and put the necklace back on. "I'll be okay in a minute."

Dad tips his head. "I'm staying right here."

Continued strength flows through my veins and muscles. "Help me up, then."

Dad's lips form a thin line, but he does as I ask.

With Dad still bracing my arm, I gather my bearings and watch as the ship burns and people from the unharmed ship help the survivors away from the wreckage.

"I'm good now." It's not the total truth but I pull away from Dad. "I have to see if I can help."

Before Dad can say anything to me, I stumble for the injured to use my Starfire on them. The idea is a longshot, but maybe I can heal these people. At the crash site, survivors are being dragged to safety. I throw myself next to the first injured woman closest to me. My stomach tightens. She's severely burned, and if I didn't see the light movement of her chest, I would think she were dead.

"It's okay, it's okay," I lie as I grab her hand. When I do, she clasps me so suddenly my heart jumps. Her eyes flick open in terror.

I grip my Starfire, and without knowing exactly what to do, I press the gem against her arm where her shirt is torn, exposing her skin. I close my eyelids to focus on the crystal's energy, the healing power I'm positive it possesses. I visualize the woman whole again and not in pain. I open my eyes to the disarray of my surroundings and the woman, who is now staring at me in wonder. She winces as she pushes up to a seated position. The burn on the side of her face is still there but is now less raw, and her breathing has returned to normal.

"Thank you," she says in a scratchy voice, bringing her fingers to her throat.

"Get farther away from here." I point to the lab. "Go there for now." I squeeze her hand and run to the next person.

Despite my body begging me to stop, I repeat the process on at least six others. And by the time I stagger to the last person, the world around me begins to swirl. I know there had to be around one hundred passengers on board the ship.

I drop next to the remaining person. My head pounds as I glance down at the lifeless body. It's a boy and he's turned on his side. I lay my hand on his shoulder and use the little strength I have left to pull him onto his back and I draw in a sharp breath. Trav. The one who helped us escape. I take in a ragged breath and try to reorient myself to focus again. But exhaustion fights me and my fatigue is winning. I can't let him die! He was probably only on the ship because of assisting us with the Rover. My breathing picks up and I grip the Starfire, but his pulse is weak.

"You can't die, you can't die," I mutter over and over again, anything to keep him alive. But it's not working, and a swirl of darkness twines around my body, lulling me into much-needed regeneration.

My mind summons for Javen. But before I can connect with him, I feel my body slump forward onto Trav's, and my mind awakens in a cyan haze.

Through the cyan, I see Javen walking toward me. Is he coming because I summoned him? I feel an intense pull on my soul to be with him. I need his help. His presence.

"Javen," I call out. But he doesn't answer, as if he can't hear me.

I flit my eyelids open to the inside of the lab. I inhale sharply and sit, eyes wide.

"Hey, it's okay," Irene's voice soothes from a chair beside me. "You're safe."

"Trav . . . what happened to Trav?" I ask as I lock onto Irene's face.

Her jaw tenses with obvious grief. "He didn't make it. A lot of people didn't make it."

A pang lances my heart. I could have saved him. My focus darts around, unable to process the loss.

I'm in the tiny sleeping quarters Dr. Owens used when he was staying here. My two bags sit in a corner and I attempt to push my legs off the bed to fetch them, but Irene plants her palm squarely on my sternum to stop me.

"Cassi," she scolds. "You pulled three ships from one dimension into another, and then you saved several people who were at death's door. Rest is the right thing for you right now."

Irene pushes me down onto the pillow.

I whisper, "At least tell me what happened."

She sighs and leans back into the chair. "We got as many people out of the damaged ship as we could. But almost everyone inside is dead. There are the ones you healed and maybe five or six others with minor wounds."

"How many died?" My stomach clenches as I ask this question.

"The ships were loaded so quickly, no one is completely sure. But probably around a hundred."

"And how many people were on the other ships?"

"Somewhere between one hundred and one hundred and twenty each. I haven't heard the final numbers."

I sit up again. "So, we have over two hundred people inside the Intersection? Do they have any supplies?" This wasn't a problem I had considered before. How are we going to care for all these refugees?

"Luckily, the two remaining ships do have a limited emergency stock of water and food. But your Dad is working on the problem since we don't know how long they're going to be in here."

"What's my Dad doing?" Sudden memories of his erratic behavior surface inside my mind.

"He's just helping them get settled for the moment and explaining as much as he can about what happened. He thinks he can use the Starfire to get their ships running again. None of the onboard tech is working. But he's not telling them that you actually pulled in the ships. Only Max and I know. He doesn't want them aware of what you are able to do."

"But they'll know I healed the wounded."

Irene frowns softly. "There was so much confusion. Even the healed aren't actually sure of what happened."

I get why my dad wants to keep my secret. If Hammond knows what I can do, it will put her on a mission to find and use me.

"Hammond's fighter ships could have seen me on the Arcadia side."

"Oh, I'm sure they saw the vessels vanish and probably have an idea that they were pulled across dimensions. But it doesn't mean they know *you* caused the event."

Tension pinches at my chest. "Then they're just going to think the Alku are responsible, which could make Hammond target them more quickly." Before Irene can stop me, I swing my legs off the bed and avoid her grasp. "I need to speak with Javen. The Alku can't be in the dark about this situation. They need to know what's happened to me and how we're using the Intersection."

"I think you need more rest. Transporting isn't a great idea right now," Irene says but doesn't try to force me back into bed.

"I feel fine now," I say. The statement isn't a complete lie. I'm still tired, but my head stopped spinning and my thoughts are clear.

"At least speak with your dad. Max told me that the leaders from the refugee ships had access to intel before you brought them to the Intersection. Let's find out what info they have before you make any rash choices. You don't want to tell the Alku anything untrue."

"Good point," I say and then head for the door.

Irene and I enter the lab and find Dad and Max in deep conversation with a man and woman I haven't met before.

Max is the first to see me and immediately leaves the group and comes to my side. A tightening, similar to resistance, settles into my chest. I hate it, but I can't seem to make the feeling stop.

"We were so worried, but Irene said she'd stay with you." I can tell by his body language that he wants to hug me but holds back instead. I have no idea whether his hesitation is because of present company or if I'm putting off vibes that are stopping him. Part of me is pained for the emotional distance, but the other part me is relieved.

I push away my feelings of confusion. There's no time to dwell on emotions right now.

"I'll be fine," I say to Max and force a smile. I turn my attention to Dad and the two others.

Dad gestures to me. "This is Cassi, my daughter . . . she helped us activate the portal, which allowed your ships to cross over to this place."

The woman, with dark skin and hair pulled away from her face, extends her hand. I take it.

"I'm General Atkins, and this is my second-in-command, Commander Tucker." She releases my hand and gestures to the man with ginger hair. "We were shocked when we found your father alive, but after so many hardships, we were glad to see him. You two have done extraordinary work here," she says. "It is a tragedy to lose our other ship and the people on board. But if your father had not opened the portal when he did, all of us would be dead."

General Atkins turns to Dad. "I was just explaining to Dr. Foster that we have custody of a video feed of intel from Hammond's headquarters. We have a spy in there. But now none of our tech will work. After we crossed into the Intersection, we had to switch the ships over to manual to land." She looks around. "But everything here seems to be working fine."

"It's all powered by the Starfire," I mutter.

"She's right," Dad says. "With the crystals, we should be able to get your ship's minimum functions up and running by tomorrow. There are Starfire fields not too far off, and it won't take much effort to harvest the needed amount."

Irene walks to the computer. "Where is the feed stored?"

Tucker raises his left hand. "I have the data on my Connect."

"Can I have it?" Irene asks.

He defers to Atkins, and she nods. Tucker releases the Connect from his wrist and hands the device to Irene. She pairs his Connect with the computer, and video immediately springs to life on the display. It's jerky from a concealed camera, but when the wearer sits, I can see they are in a meeting that's about to begin.

On the display, Hammond walks into the room followed by Luca, as if he were her pet on a leash. I grit my teeth together.

"Mining is set to begin immediately," Hammond says, now standing at the head of the group. "We have the full support of the World Senate, and with our newly improved Inhibitor, we have been able to push back on the Alku's Starfire energy usage that was meant to block us from mining."

Atkins sighs and then straightens her shoulders. "This video feed was taken right before the attack on our ships. Hammond's ships took out the last of our defense in Primaro after we escaped the city. At that point, we knew we were goners but still hoped to reach the Tahms. We've heard rumors that a few of the World Senate members who support us may still be alive and are willing to get word back to Earth for reinforcements through the Turner Space Fold. Help could exit closer to Arcadia and possibly be here in a few days. The hope for assistance was slim but worth exploring."

"So, these World Senate members are hiding somewhere on Arcadia?" Max asks.

"If the rumors are true," Tucker answers.

"Then people who oppose Hammond are hiding them," Dad says.

"And we need to find them," I add.

I look back to the video display Irene paused. Right behind Luca is another face I recognize.

Alina.

Alina is working for Hammond.

My heart drops into my stomach as I replay in my mind the last time I met her in Primaro. She pulled me away from the soldier bots and off the street. Why? If she's working with Hammond, then she must have wanted information from me. But she didn't ask me anything. I rack my brain to remember what happened. The only thing I can recall is how I nearly dropped my bag and she helped me.

"I'm not feeling well again," I say to get out of the lab. "I'd like to go lie down."

"Do you need any help?" Dad asks.

I wave my hand in the air as I turn. "No. I'll be okay."

Dad nods and asks Irene to continue playing the video.

Max follows me to the door and stops me on the other side of it. "What's going on, Cassi?"

I glimpse the concern on his face, but then I quickly study the ground. "There's obviously a lot to do. Before I'm going to be of any more use to anyone, I need to get some rest. I was wrong earlier when I said I felt okay." I chance a look his way. "But I'll be fine in a few hours."

Max squeezes my arm and lets loose. "You would tell me if something else was going on, right?"

I lock eyes with him and whisper, "Yes."

He nods and returns to the lab. But I get the feeling that he knows I'm lying.

When the door shuts, I race to the sleeping quarters and grab for my messenger bag. I throw open the top and dig inside for Dad's journal. But it's gone. Did Alina take it when I wasn't looking? I expel a short breath in frustration. Honestly, I don't even know what is scribbled on the pages. Dr. Owens thought the journal might just be a personal log. But I don't want to worry Dad by asking him. I pace the room, but there's nothing I can do now. Hammond either has the journal or she doesn't.

I fumble for my Starfire pendant. Holding the crystal calms me immediately, and my mind drifts to Javen. I must speak to him and relay any information I know, as well as admit to him the truth of the Intersection.

A wave of pressure moves through my body, and I open my eyes to daylight. My heart leaps as I spot Javen only feet in front of me. His face lights up when he sees me, and my heart calls for him. But I take one step in his direction and a boom sounds, shaking the ground and knocking me off my feet.

Chapter 18

race to Javen's embrace and melt into his arms. "Was that a bomb or an earthquake?" I ask.

"A quake, but they're very rare in this area."

Overhead, the sky has changed, almost as if the shaking of the ground cracked the atmosphere.

I step away from Javen a few inches. "Hammond began harvesting from the Starfire mines. Could the mining cause earthquakes?"

Javen tenses his jaw. "Very little information is coming back from Arcadia to Paxon. Our people have been completely driven from the city and blocked from the mining area. I warned my father this would happen, but he won't listen. He refuses to use the Starfire as a weapon, even to protect our people. He fears that, even if we prevail, the risk is too high and we may grow aggressive toward other Alku."

"But isn't that what's already happening between Vihann and Wirrin's group? Beda is totally aggressive."

"Wirrin's group is small compared to the Alku who follow my father. And at this point, they will likely lose to Hammond. My father knows this."

Shock trembles down my arms, and I step back farther from him. "And your father would allow the Alku to die?"

"He will."

Anger simmers in my core. "I don't understand the benefit. Hammond isn't going to use the Starfire for beneficial reasons. Why won't Vihann take a chance in fighting her to keep the Alku from dying? There are still moral people out there who might be able to stop the massacre."

Curling my hands into fists, I tell Javen about the World Senate assassinations and how some of the Senators are missing. "So, there's a chance they're hiding in Arcadia. If the Alku attempt to remove Hammond from power, we may be able to swing back favor from those in the Senate who are only afraid of losing their lives and the lives of their families."

"Cassi, but you don't even know if any of the missing Senators are actually alive. And even if a few are, will they be able to call on assistance from anyone on Earth?"

I know his words are true. "That is why the Alku need to fight. You are here, and you are our best chance." I plant my feet and lock stares with Javen. "You are the future leader of the Alku. I understand why your father feels the way he does. It's a huge risk, but one worth taking."

Javen tucks his hands into his pockets and looks to the ground. I know he must feel torn between two worlds—two groups of people.

"The One Pure Soul was willing to take a risk for your people—to save them."

Javen tips his head slightly in interest at what I have to say.

"This situation is different, but we can use the Starfire power for good and save two worlds."

"The One Pure Soul story is lore for children," he says, shaking his head.

"I've seen this middle dimension. I also believe your father and Wirrin, as well as many other leaders before them, have been hiding the truth of the Intersection to protect your people. And for good reason. It's more powerful and complicated than any of us know. I pulled three ships boarded by hundreds of people who were escaping Hammond into the Intersection."

"By yourself?" His face scrunches up with confusion.

"With the help of *this* Starfire." I pull the gem from under my collar. Javen touches the crystal in my fingers and his irises swirl. He inhales deeply and releases.

"This crystal is different."

"The Starfire from the Intersection is the source of the crystals on either side. This type connects them." As the words escape my mouth, I am filled with a strong desire to be with Javen and my heart pulses audibly in my ears. "Like our bond."

Relief fills his eyes as his irises return to brown again. "I felt you slipping from me while we were apart."

Heat travels up my neck at the reminder of my and Max's kiss. "Javen, if the rest of the Alku people share the same heart as you do, then we can do this . . . together. I believe the Starfire in the Intersection is going to allow our people to live in harmony, if we just use the energy correctly. We need to bring your father and Wirrin together."

Javen caresses my cheek, and a burst of electricity trails down my spine. "I know you speak truth."

"Would your father come if you summoned him?" I ask.

"Despite my urging, he remains clear on his stance to be neutral."

"But if you go to him in person and tell him of the new information—would he come?"

Javen tips his head to me. "Possibly. And if he won't, I will summon the rest of my people." Javen squares his shoulders. "I am their future leader, and some may follow me now."

Pride wells up within me. My lips curl into a smile at his newfound determination, and I reach up to kiss him. The second my lips touch his, he snakes his arms around my waist and gathers me close to his muscled chest. Reality fades and stars fill my vision. The need to be close to him aches from depths of myself I never knew existed. As if to mirror my feelings, he rakes his hands into my hair, bringing me even closer as I reach under his untucked shirt to touch the soft skin of his lower back. Javen shivers at the touch. I kiss him deeply and breathe in his warm breath, wishing we could stay like this forever in our universe of two. But I know we can't.

As if he knows it, too, he releases me and then looks me straight in the eye, panting.

"Cassiopeia Foster. I realize that what we feel might only be from the Starfire."

I step away from him, shocked that he may be having the same feelings I am.

"I was lying to myself when I said I didn't. Since we've been separated, I've felt the Starfire bond diminish. And I know you have questions and doubts. And there is another you may have feelings for."

I open my mouth to speak.

"But true commitment is not based on something external . . . our connection can't only be about the Starfire. I need to know this bond is also from your heart."

My thoughts wander to my kiss with Max. Part of that felt so right, too. I like Max so much and never want to hurt him because of a moment of weakness. A flush spreads up my chest and neck. "Don't you still have feelings for Yaletha?"

Javen sighs. "I do. She's a brave, intelligent and strong young woman—"

"And beautiful," I interrupt.

"Yes." He grazes the hair hanging over my forehead with his fingertips. "But I've also seen *you*, and *you* are brave, intelligent and strong . . . and so beautiful. I've seen your past and desire to be a part of your future." He lowers his voice to a hoarse whisper and says, "I've touched your soul, Cassiopeia. My soul is determined to belong with yours."

I swallow the lump in my throat and my breathing picks up.

"I will save my people and Paxon, and I will prove that my love for you is stronger than the Starfire connecting us."

Nerves builds in my chest, hot and searing. "You . . . you *love* me?"

He chuckles. "Do you think I would be able to say all that if I didn't? You are the one person I want to spend my life with. I'm certain you will lead Paxon and the Alku people with me. But I will never force you to feel the same about me or choose this future."

Deep respect for Javen floods my heart, more than I've ever known for another person. "I have so many questions."

His lips spread into a small smile. "I know you do, and I hope to help you find the answers."

Unable to hold my desire for him back any longer, I rise on my toes and slip my hand around his neck and into his thick hair. My lips find his and move in a breathless, languid dance against his mouth. I want to remain here in Javen's arms longer. But instead, I drop back to my heels and clear my throat. "I need to reach Wirrin before Beda convinces him to do something rash." I look around me, only seeing an open field surrounded by trees, and realize I have no idea where we are or where Wirrin's group is.

"Where is your uncle?"

Javen looks down at the ground. "I believe the army is going to the largest mining site on Arcadia to regain control."

I gnaw on my lower lip as fear shoots down my spine. If Hammond has started mining, the site will be heavily guarded, and she'll be using the Inhibitors. Panic zips through my veins. "They are heading to their deaths. I need to stop Wirrin before he reaches the mining fields."

"I'll summon you after I speak with my father again." He pauses for a moment, as if thinking. "If you let your mind direct you to Wirrin while you transport, the Starfire should take you to him."

'Thank you." I skim his hand with the tips of my fingers and close my eyes, focusing on the mining site's location as I remember it from my Earthscape program. At the same time, I reach out to Wirrin as if summoning him. Hopefully, with my limited experience, the process will work.

I open my eyes and Javen is gone. I seem to have ended up on the side of a hill, and below is the mining site. I duck into the safety of a few low-growing plants and watch the activity below. Most of the Starfire on Arcadia is buried under the earth, unlike how they grow on Paxon. Small fields are closer to the surface, but most are farther down. The crystals are delicate and will need to be dug out primarily by hand . . . either human or bot.

Groups of people mill around near several large ships, which are parked beside the site. In the center of the mining operation is a significant hole, where digging efforts appear to be concentrated. Three large patrol ships fly above. I sweep my gaze over the terrain in search of Wirrin and his group, but I don't see them. Then, to my right, maybe three hundred yards away, I spot a cyan glow. A glow similar to that produced when Javen cloaked me from others. I have no idea why I can see the illumination. My link to the Starfire must be allowing the transparency. It also means, at least at this distance from the mines, that the Alku are able to use the energy.

I touch the Starfire around my neck and attempt to cloak myself. Waves of energy flow through me and I grow lightheaded. But a telltale faint cyan glow circles my body. Now the ships above and the miners below can't spot me. I race for Wirrin's group, who are now completely visible to me. Maybe one hundred Alku form the group. How do they plan to go up against Hammond's Inhibitor and her ships with so few?

A half-dozen Alku soldiers tense as I approach, but no one makes a move to stop me. I have the feeling many of them remember me from the meeting I had with Vihann and the Council. They know the Starfire chose me and, despite their differences with Vihann, will not challenge the will of the Starfire by harming me. At least, that's my hope.

Wirrin steps to the front of the group, Beda at his side. "Why are you here, Cassi?" he asks. He must see the argument in my eyes, even several feet away. Straightening his shoulders, he takes another step forward. "I can't stand by any longer. Someone must stop Hammond from stripping the Starfire from Arcadia."

Panting, I stop several feet in front of him. I glance at Beda and then back to Wirrin. "Of course. But your tiny band of warriors will never win. Hammond has tech you've never encountered."

I look back to the mines and tilt my head. Why are there so few ships guarding the production crew?

"You're walking into a trap. Hammond wants the Alku to splinter. If you challenge her today, then you're doing exactly what she wants."

Beda marches forward and stops inches from my face. "The Alku will not go down without a fight."

"Then fight smart," I say without backing down. "We need to figure out how Hammond is blocking the Starfire's energy and take *that* out first. Then we can hit them." I spot Yaletha hanging at the back of the group. She's one of the best soldiers, so of course she'd be here. The beautiful Alku warrior holds my gaze for a moment and then breaks away and returns her attention to the impending battle.

A blast thunders from behind, and I whip toward the sound. The shaft created to dig out the ore is now larger. And then the earth quakes again.

This time, I not only feel the vibration under my feet but also inside of me. Like part of my soul is being decimated.

Beda winces, as do the rest of the Alku. They feel the agony, too.

"You see what the mining is doing?" Wirrin points to the shaft as a scowl appears between his eyebrows. "The digging is upsetting the balance of the Intersection. And it will kill us one way or another. We can't wait."

He pushes me aside and yells for his small army to advance. Rushing toward the mine in frenzied waves, the Alku flood around me, leaving me behind.

I watch in horror, and as they approach the mine, the pressure builds in my chest as if I might explode, too. Then, in a single frantic heartbeat, the Starfire's haze, the energy cloaking them from view, shifts. Each of their hands glows bright cyan, almost electric, just like when Javen blasted out of the window in the Capitol building during our escape.

I watch, frozen in place, as the three ships swoop in and release a swarm of silver bots from the hull's underside. Everything in me wants to turn away when the bots descend on the Alku.

Shadows from the ships pass over the scattering miners. The people run in every direction like herds of cattle escaping an incoming predator.

The Alku hurl blue-green lights at the AI, and metal explodes in the air. But there are too many. I watch in confusion as the bots don't attack. The AI only fly in and out of the Alku, like a swarm of bugs.

I gasp as Wirrin's group reaches the mine to begin their attack, but the miners are retreating.

My Connect buzzes, and a hologram pops up above the surface.

"Breaking news," the text reads, and the hologram fills with angry-looking Alku who charge on the helpless, unarmed miners.

The bots are cameras! Hammond lured the Alku here to create propaganda and justify her argument that they are evil.

"No, Hammond," I grit under my breath. "*You* are the evil one."

Chapter 19

gape from the hillside, stunned. The Alku still move toward the mining operation, and the camera bots scatter back to the safety of the ships above, like a swarm of bees returning to their hive.

Some of the Alku hurl glowing orbs of light toward the mining machines and they explode. A ship circling above lands near the mine, and soldiers and soldier bots pour from the hatch, weapons extended.

Another ship swoops in and hovers over the Alku. Several of them hurl light orbs at the ship, but their attack yields little damage. Then the floating ship shudders slightly as a white glow extends from the hull.

A shiver crawls over my body, intensifying when the Alku's glowing energy dissipates. Hammond has the footage she needs now, and so they have reactivated the Starfire Inhibitor. The Alku are defenseless, and the soldiers are going to shoot them. The citizens of Primaro aren't out here to witness this battle, and Hammond will declare the massacre was in self-defense, if anything is reported at all.

The slight glow from cloaking myself is still visible around me. The Inhibitor isn't affecting the Starfire energy from this distance. My throat tightens, and I clench my fists, knowing what I need to do. After pulling the escape ships across the Intersection earlier, using the ability now could harm me further or even kill me. But I must try.

I touch my crystal necklace and home in on the Alku who have now stopped . . . even the several who are now retreating. But Beda, Wirrin, and Yaletha hold their ground. I have no idea if the three are in shock or just that stubbornly brave.

I don't know if this will work since Javen couldn't cross with me into the Intersection the first time. Still, I hold up my hands and trace an area in my mind around the entire group of Alku. I visualize the location I need to bring them to within the Intersection. I could be wrong, but since the Alku can't transport in on their own, I don't think they can transport out. I summon Wirrin's army to my mind. Then, with everything in me, I force every bit of energy I have toward each Alku. My body rips with pain as if I'm exploding, and light discharges from me in bright beams.

It's as if I am everywhere and nowhere, gathering the last of the Alku and forcing them through the portal.

It's as if a thousand knives are trying to rip me apart to do so.

I grit down and focus my mind. My body tumbles into the Intersection's still darkness, skidding and scraping over the rocky ground. The Alku appear and fall to the ground as I release them from my energy.

My vision blurs, but I spot the three ally ships, the one downed and burned, and then . . .

Everything goes black.

△ △ △

My consciousness fades in and out, but my body jostles, as if being carried.

"She needs help. The Starfire isn't healing her," the voice says, and I struggle to identify who is speaking. I lift my head up and start. Beda. The last person I ever thought would be attempting to help me. I must be hallucinating. But before I question anything, darkness sweeps over me.

I blink my eyes open once again. The sleeping area in the lab comes in and out of focus. This time, instead of Irene's face, I see Beda watching me. I open my mouth to speak but nothing comes out, and my body shudders with a barrage of chills. The room is freezing, a sensation I haven't felt since arriving on Arcadia. An Alku woman with dark skin and long white hair pulled into a side braid appears from Beda's side and leans over me, pulling open my eyelids. By now my teeth are chattering from the ice-cold room.

"C–can I have a blanket?" I manage to stutter.

"You already have three," Beda says in a surprisingly calm voice. "There aren't any more."

I fixate on not passing out again, but the room spins and I feel as if I could turn into ice any second. "Wha– what's wrong with me?" I choke out.

The white-haired woman grazes my forehead with her fingers. "You have experienced some of the most intense Starfire exposure I've ever seen, my dear." The corners of her lips curl into a kind smile. "Your body is just trying to figure out what to do with the energy."

My mind carousels. I have no idea if that is a good or bad thing. She could be smiling at me only because I'm going to die at any moment. I grit my teeth against their chattering and sudden pain shoots up my back like electric bolts.

"She's awake?" Dad's voice travels to me from outside the room, and then he appears in the doorway. His jaw is tense, and he pushes past Yaletha, who stands guard near the door. Max and Irene attempt to do the same, but she stops them with her arm and an intense stare.

"I was so worried about you, Cassi." Dad kneels next to me and takes my hand.

"Dr. Foster," the female Alku says. "There is nothing you can do here. This is Alku business."

Dad furrows his eyebrows and twists his gaze toward her. "My daughter, my business."

"Fine," she says. "You may have a word. But I need to continue the process."

My heart jumps, and I lock eyes with Dad. "Process? What process?"

He takes my hand and squeezes my palm. "No one will tell me, but I believe these Alku are helping you, Cassi."

"You must leave now, Dr. Foster," the white-haired woman says.

Dad winces and squeezes my hand. "I'll be right outside if you need me."

I want to tell Dad I love him, but my tongue refuses as the world spins again. Seconds later, I feel the Alku enter my mind and the Starfire's energy flow through them and into me. Their presence and control of the power gradually settles the sensations inside me, as if they're taking in part of the overflow. The passing time is irrelevant—minutes, hours, or even days. It could be any amount of time.

Cyan dreams once again fill my mind. And this time, I'm soaring over Paxon, through lush hills and valleys, over mountains and the clearest oceans and most beautiful white-sand beaches I've ever seen. This place is pristine, unlike most of Earth's landscapes, many of which have been ravaged. My lungs fill with the clean air, refreshing my soul. Ahead, I spot a series of structures that are nestled inside a valley. Somehow, I know it's the community where Javen lives—where he was born. As I reach the center, my consciousness flutters from the sky and drops down, leading me to a single structure.

But immediately the wonder I feel is dashed.

"What's wrong?" a familiar, lyrical male voice asks. I know he's speaking in the Alku tongue. But my mind translates the words.

I don't even know who this is, but the question makes my core twist with worry.

My bodiless self flows through the walls of the Alku home. In the main living area stands a young Vihann with his hands on his head. Deep frown lines stretch across his face.

A youthful version of the woman who is healing me in the lab stands in front of Vihann with an equally worried expression. She paces the room. "The birth progressed successfully—"

Am I seeing the time after Javen was born? He doesn't have any siblings that I know of. Did something go wrong?

"—but after Zarah deteriorated," the woman continues, "the Starfire energy left her body suddenly. And when the energy returned in a blast of light? It was as if the shift changed her. Her eyes went blank."

"I don't care what you say. I must see her, Analya," Vihann demands, and then pushes past her and races out the door.

I tail the two of them wherever they are going. I must know what happened to Javen's mother. He's never mentioned her, and I don't understand why. And why had I never thought to ask? The guilt over my insensitivity toward him weighs on me.

Vihann ends at another structure, and I follow him and Analya inside.

"You shouldn't have brought him here," a male Alku I don't know says.

"I couldn't stop him." Analya places her hand on the man's shoulder. "He needs to see for himself."

I follow Vihann into a room and ahead of him is a woman, lying in a pillow-like bed. Her dark hair spreads out in soft waves over the top of the bed. To our left is a white-haired female Alku with a newborn infant in her arms, nursing him.

"You have a son, Vihann," she says.

He bows his head to her. "Thank you for acting as a nursemaid," Vihann mumbles.

Barely looking at his son, he returns his attention to the woman on the bed, his wife, and kneels on the floor beside her and takes her hand. Quietly he sobs as she moans but doesn't wake.

"Her condition has not changed," Analya says. "And the Starfire is blocking me from seeing into her mind. Until the energy releases her, I'm unsure if her condition will improve."

"But how can you know this?"

"You know I'm unable to be one hundred percent certain," Analya says.

"But you are rarely wrong." Vihann rises slowly and releases Zarah's hand. "I need a few moments with my son." He gently takes Javen from the nursemaid's arms and exits the room. The others follow behind, leaving me alone with Javen's mother.

I float over to her and settle to her side. Zarah's skin is pale and her cheeks hollow. My heart sinks. Did Javen's mother die after this? "What happened to you?" I say.

Without warning, the woman sits up and looks straight at me, her eyes swirling with cyan.

I flinch and try to back away, but something holds me in place. Zarah tips her head and raises her hand to graze her fingers against my cheek, as if I had a real body. The touch vibrates against me.

"It's time for you to return to the others," she says." But you must forget what you've seen here—for now."

I don't want to forget! I begin to speak and tell her "No," but then she touches my forehead. The sadness and memories start to dissipate, and peace streams through me instead. My body finally relaxes, and I open my eyes to the room in the lab. The last thing I remember is a woman helping me to heal. Beda leans back in the chair beside my bed, her legs outstretched and her arms crossed over her chest, asleep.

But the second I sit up, her eyes pop open.

"Why are you here with me?" I ask before she can say anything. "Is Wirrin forcing you again?"

For the first time since I met Beda, she actually doesn't bristle against my question.

She presses her lips together in thought. Then she looks down and whispers, "I was wrong about you." Her demeanor quickly changes. She looks me straight in the eyes and speaks, her voice full. "I was wrong about you."

At first, I don't know what to say. The lack of bristling and glaring confuses me. "What . . . do you mean?" I definitely think Beda *has* been wrong about me, but I know that her heart was to protect her people. I've always known this.

"When the humans arrived, my people shifted. Our focus was no longer about caring only for ourselves. Vihann's and the Council's philosophy was that we should be willing to share the Starfire, if needed. Doing so would help us atone for the violence in our past and allow the Alku to use the gifts our planet had. But I didn't like this. People, and not just Alku, made peace more difficult. Humans and Alku do not always share the same values. How would we ever get along? The Alku have been at peace for centuries."

"And our being here put your peace at risk."

"Exactly. Then we were proved right when Hammond decided to mass mine the Starfire on Arcadia."

"But all that *is* happening. Your father and Vihann are still at odds, and Hammond is mining."

Beda glances away again. "When you saved us, your mind joined with ours."

"I summoned you."

She shakes her head slowly. "No, greater than summoning. Deeper. I saw you; we all did. I saw into your heart, Cassi. Human or not, you are as pure as Javen said. I just didn't want to believe him. Despite our mistakes . . . *my* mistakes, you've seen our desire to maintain the Alku way of life. What we truly want is unity among my people."

"And it's not what you have right now."

"No, and this discord is making us crazy." She leans her head into her hands.

"You know, I kinda hated you," I admit.

Beda opens her fingers and peeks through them at me. "You should have." She lowers her hands and sits straight. "But you still didn't give up on us, despite how I was treating you. You also showed us what Hammond was doing with all those"—She waves her hand in the air— "flying things."

"The camera bots?"

"Yes. Hammond will use our attack to prove her claim of the Alku's aggressive nature. It's how she'll make digging up the Starfire appear honorable before the humans."

I want to be relieved at her admission. But we still haven't solved the bigger issues. I push off the bed, and as I do, my legs wobble like jelly. And something is missing, but I can't pinpoint what.

"What happened to me?" I touch my neck for the Starfire and find nothing.

"The crystal is gone. For now," she says.

"What? Why? Without it, I can't transport."

"There's nothing my mother could do. The Starfire energy needs to settle in you. Transporting the three ships and then all of us could have killed you. She has never seen or heard of any Alku doing anything similar.

Especially not when we are first learning to control the energy in our bodies."

"Your mother?" I knit my brows together.

"The woman who healed you is my mother, Analya."

My mind is so cloudy, but hazy memories resurface. And I see her in my mind's eye. Analya, the woman with the braided white hair. "So, you carried me here, *and* your mother saved me— ironic, when you hated me before."

A humble expression crosses Beda's face. "Saving you was our privilege." Her lips turn into a devious smile. "But . . . I am still considerably stronger than you. I wouldn't push it."

I chuckle. "Point taken. Now, would you please help me to find the others? I can't lie here all day. I'll go crazy."

Chapter 20

Beda supports me, keeping my weak legs from collapsing from underneath me as we make our way through the lab's hallways. But no one seems to be here.

"They must be outside," Beda says. "The Alku, your father, and the other refugees have been working nonstop to set up camp as well as figure out a way for us to transport out of the Intersection."

I glance at her. So my hunch was right "You can't transport from here?"

Beda frowns. "No, several of us tried and failed. We can't even summon anyone outside of the Intersection. There's no communication in or out. As of now, the link seems to be only with you."

"And I can't transport right now." Keeping the Alku here until we can come up with a different plan is good, but disappointment still seeps into my stomach. I still can't reach Javen to see if he has spoken with his father, and we have no idea where Hammond is in the mining process, or whether the Alku outside of the Intersection are safe.

"The leaders are trying to figure out an alternative method that will allow us to transport the group as well as the two refugee ships."

"My dad's project," I say.

Beda nods and leads me toward the exit, and already my legs have gained a bit of strength.

"I want to try walking on my own now." I unhook from her arm.

"I think you're going to be surprised by how fast everything is moving." She activates the door, and my breath grows short as my eyes try to settle on all the activity outside in the night air. The entire area is bustling, with Alku and human refugees working together. The two functional escape ships float over the ground in the distance, both illuminated by the blue-green cast of Starfire energy. Organic structures that look similar to the buildings in Irilee have also been fashioned to house everyone.

"How did all this happen so fast?" I ask.

She hands me a protein bar from her pocket. "Well, you were healing over the last several days. But the Starfire energy has the ability to manifest our housing and items we need with the help of the Alku. We made the homes for the survivors."

My mouth slacks open and my eyes widen, but she doesn't blink an eye at my surprise at both statements. This must have to do with how Dad was generating items in the Intersection like the apples. He just didn't know how he did it.

Beda waves me forward. "Let me take you to our fathers."

I study Beda's face. The constant scowl I've known, ever since the first time I met her on the streets of Primaro, is absent and instead is replaced by an expression glimmering with hope. Her soft, brown eyes are filled with excitement and expectation even though all could be lost outside of the Intersection. Beda is truly beautiful when she feels like the resources to save her people are within her grasp. I follow her past a scattering of Alku and humans who are busy working toward whatever our next steps will be. A few of the people we pass are holding containers of Starfire.

Beda points to a hill on our left. "Over the hill is a Starfire field. My mother has been helping everyone harvest a sample of mature crystals to use. The power the Starfire from this dimension have is amazing. The field is where I'm taking you."

My chest constricts. I still think we risk the Starfire from this place becoming all-consuming and we need to be cautious. That was the risk of bringing anyone here. I hope Dad has made sure the Alku and refugees understand this drawback . . . if even he knows. Still, he seems to have returned to his former self—no more strange behavior.

I eat my bar and pocket the wrapper while Beda picks up our pace toward the hill's summit. My lungs struggle for breath from the climb. Leaning over my knees, drawing in deep breaths, I spot the field, and the soft glow from the sea of crystals takes my heaving breath away. Of course, I knew the crystals were here, since Dad gave me one. If I thought the field on Paxon was beautiful, that sight is nothing compared to this expanse.

The field pulses as if to different beats, and a low hum accompanies the vibrations at various tones. And although I had grown used to the almost musical tone of the Alku's voices, seeing and hearing these crystals reminds me of the Alku's lyrical quality again. I shiver when recalling Javen's beautiful voice, and the longing to return to him tugs mercilessly at my heart.

Beda grabs me by the shoulder, releasing me from my thoughts. "The meeting is down here." She gestures to the field's right, where I spot a small gathering. As we move closer, I make out Dad, Wirrin, Analya, and General Atkins in company with a few others who are unfamiliar to me.

"Where are Max and Irene?" I ask.

"They're assisting the two refugee ships," Beda says. "Both vessels contain a limited amount of defense capability, and Irene is helping to link the computer system to the Starfire power. Apparently, it's going well."

When I draw closer to the group, Dad spots me. "Cassi. Thank goodness." Relief washes over his face and he rushes to my side, throwing his arms around me. "Analya kept reassuring me that you would pull through as the Starfire hadn't permanently damaged you." He pulls away, holds me at arm's length and then looks me over. "But I had to see you with my own eyes to be sure." When I don't speak, Dad loosens his grasp on my upper arms. "You are okay, right?"

"I think so." Any other time I would want to share my experience with him, but there's no time for any of that. "What are you planning?"

Dad returns his attention to the group and then gestures for Beda and me to follow him. Yaletha steps forward and I want to be jealous of her like I was before. But I can't. She glances at me briefly and then flits her attention toward the crystals.

"After speaking to Wirrin," Dad says, cutting through my thoughts, "we plan to open a large portal, enough to allow the two ships as well as the Alku resistance back through to the other side. Most of the refugees will stay back here unless military-trained.

Using the newly upgraded ships, we will then create a distraction so the Alku can move in and destroy the device Hammond uses to depress the Starfire energy."

"But how will you be able to use the refugee ships if the energy is blocked?" I ask.

"I've run the terrain through the Earthscape program," he says. "We've tested the firing distance of the new weapons, and I've also been able to estimate the range of the Inhibitor Hammond is using."

"But she had airborne ships with Inhibitors the last time," I say, "moving them toward the source of unwanted energy."

"Before we execute our mission, we'll send a few individuals through to retrieve information," Wirrin says.

"We're hoping our spy is still alive and can provide intel on how the Inhibitor is being used. There was talk of one device being permanently installed at the mine," General Atkins says.

"Your friend Irene believes she can shut down the computer technology used by the humans by doing something called . . ." Wirrin looks to Analya for help.

"Hacking . . . she called it hacking," Analya reminds him.

"Yes, hacking," Wirrin says. "She says by hacking she'll create a disruption in the mine's communication, allowing us to stop mining operations with as few casualties as possible."

I look from Wirrin to Dad. "And what will I be doing? Right now, I can't help with any of those plans."

Beda steps forward. "That's not where we need your help. Irene found something your father and you both need to attend to."

"I don't want her to come," Dad says. "She's healing and can stay here."

"This is Cassi's fight, too," Beda presses.

"Come where?" I look at Dad.

He sighs. "Irene finally gave me Matt Owens's belongings. Among them was encoded information on the World Senate. Members who were die-hard loyalists to Hammond and Hirata, as well as the people on the fence. The information perfectly coincides with the intel General Atkins has on the members who were executed, the ones who migrated to Hammond—"

"I'm sure some of them did so to save themselves," I say.

"Likely," Dad quickly replies.

"What about your team, though?"

"Apparently, after the explosion, Hammond wouldn't release information about my disappearance. So, Owens went underground, so to speak. From his notes, he tried to convince the rest of my team to do the same. But Jonas and Abbot resisted, wanting to continue our work.

They believed they could handle Hammond since we always had before."

"But it didn't happen," I say.

"Matt saw through how she was using my disappearance—or death, as far as he was concerned—to go in another direction politically."

"Good for him."

"Owens, however, was always the most suspicious of her on my team. Apparently, he broke off with the rest, telling them he needed time for a mental health break because of my death and witnessing the explosion. The excuse was accepted, and he used the opportunity to use the lab. But he also had a contact who was helping to cover all his tracks."

"Do we know who?"

"No," Dad says. "But there's a possibility this group or person is doing the same thing for the missing Senate members. We need to find them as soon as we can."

"So, the MIA Senate members can get help from Earth, if they haven't already done so."

"Yes." Dad nods. "That's exactly what we need to do." He looks back to the Alku and the others in the group. "The Starfire and these ship upgrades will not be ready to cross over for at least another twenty-four hours. But I believe we can initiate a small portal for a few of us to cross over to find Owens's contact. I think if the World Senate members in hiding learn that I'm alive, the survivors may follow me. I wasn't the highest-ranking member of the Board, but I was still a Board member."

"Your crossing over to Arcadia was not part of the agreement." Wirrin steps up to Dad as his eyes swirl with cyan. From my and Wirrin's previous conversation, I know that he was concerned about the Starfire's effects on Dad. I was, too. But Dad has returned to his usual self, and thankfully, I don't see the crystals negatively affecting anyone else. It seems quite the opposite, in fact. Maybe Wirrin and I were wrong.

I touch Wirrin's forearm. "I understand your concern. But look around . . . there's nothing to validate your worries. Humans and Alku are working together better than ever. The Intersection Starfire can be used for good. We can use these crystals together to take back Paxon and Arcadia. We *can* live in peace. And my dad is right. We need to shock these Senate members into remembering who they are and what is right. These people believe my father is dead. Seeing him again will remind them that standing up to Hammond isn't impossible."

Wirrin presses his lips into a thin line, then nods.

"We'll be back before the primary launch."

I pull Beda aside. "I need for you to come with us. I can't cloak myself, and it's something we may need to find Owens's contact."

She purses her lips. "You'll have to find someone else. I'm needed here. I volunteered to be one of the first in at the mine. And there are preparations to be made."

I pull away from her, stunned. "You know that's likely to get you killed."

Beda sets her jaw and doesn't answer for a second. "I'm not afraid to give my life for my people. We knew the attack before was likely suicide, but we were unwilling to go down without a fight. It's the same this time, but the plan is better. There is a chance for success, for peace. I want to be a part of *that*."

I sigh. "Then cross with us and summon Javen. I need to know if he was able to gather any more Alku to fight—"

"With or without Vihann's permission?" she interrupts.

"If Vihann wouldn't agree, then Javen was going to stand up as the future leader and summon his people into action."

A proud expression falls over Beda's face. "I will cross with you and stay until Javen arrives. But I must return after he does."

I look at Dad. "We need to do this as soon as possible."

Analya's face takes on a pinched expression, and she lays her hand on my sternum and closes her eyes. She takes in a long breath. I feel the tingle of her Starfire energy throughout my body, and when she opens her eyes, the irises swirl with color.

"You are healing quickly. More quickly than I would have expected," she says. "But you are still not ready to use the Starfire."

I consider my body, and somehow, I know what she says is true. "How will I know?"

"You will know."

I bow my head slightly and internally hope I won't need to use Starfire energy before that time.

Dad clasps Wirrin's upper arm and nods to the rest of the group. "You know what to do. We'll return as soon as we can." He gestures to Beda and me.

"I have a few things to take care of first." Beda glances at her parents and then me. "I'll meet you at the lab in a few minutes."

"Don't be long." I wave to her and then allow Dad to lead me from the group.

"When you are ready again, I have it." Dad leans into me and pats his shirt pocket.

"What?" I ask.

"Your Starfire."

"Thanks, Dad." I close my eyes and take a deep breath in preparation for the words I'm about to admit. "Dr. Owens ... he gave me a leather journal that belonged to you."

Dad's eyes light up. "Where is it?"

My stomach twists into a knot, knowing what I have to say. "I lost it . . . your journal may have been stolen."

"Stolen? How?" He stops walking and faces me.

"It's a long story, but I think I trusted the wrong person, and they may have taken it."

"And you can't get it back?"

"I don't think so."

Dad starts walking again. "That was your mother's journal."

"Mom's?"

"She wrote in the pages every day after visiting Arcadia for the first time. Which means she wrote in it right up until she died." Sadness creeps into his voice.

"What did she write about?" I ask as the lab comes into view.

"I don't know. She never shared her journal with me, and I didn't have the key. I guess I could have tried harder, but I didn't have the guts to read her words after she died."

I twist her gold ring on my finger with my thumb. And now Hammond probably has Mom's journal, pried the lock open, and read my mom's private thoughts. "I'm sorry I was so careless."

Dad turns to me. "Cassi, I never expect you to be perfect." He reaches for the palm scanner near the door. The device beeps, and the door slides away. Irene stands on the other side and lifts an eyebrow.

She smiles when she recognizes me. "I came to check on you, but you were gone."

"I'm glad you're here, Irene," Dad says. "I need your help manning the program."

Beda runs up and joins us as Dad ushers us all into the lab. Inside, there's a clear container of Starfire next to one of the computers, and to the side, an experiment of some sort is happening with more crystals. I wrinkle my brows and lean in closer. A beaker is partially filled with what looks like cyan-colored water, but it must be a liquified piece of Starfire.

Beda hands me a laser pistol. "You may need this."

"Thanks," I whisper and shove the gun into the back of my pants under my shirt.

"Load up the portal program," Dad says to Irene.

She activates the holographic display, and her fingers fly over the keys.

"Configure the settings to open on Arcadia for three travelers." Dad retrieves a black device, the one on the table I noticed from previous visits, and then places it in his pocket. "Leave the entry open. I can activate the portal from Arcadia when we need to return. Beda will be doing a turnaround."

A crackling sound sparks from behind as the room lights up in brighter blue-green. I turn and spot an electronic portal on the opposite side of the lab.

Dad eyes Beda and me. "You two ready?"

I tilt my head at Dad and cock an eyebrow. "I think the question is—Are *you* ready? Because stepping through to Arcadia brings you back from the dead."

Chapter 21

Javen appears before us, and his eyes immediately flit to Beda. He tips his head with a quizzical look, as if sensing something has changed within her.

She gives him a tight smile, turns to the still-active portal and walks back through the opening. After she disappears, the crackling and glow of the opening fades into nothing.

My heart skips and I hurry to him, taking his hand. His smile is warm like sunshine and the heat of his gaze flushes through me. I kiss him on the cheek and then bring his attention to Dad before Javen decides to deepen our affection. And then I freeze, remembering myself. *I kissed his cheek in front of Dad!*

"This is my dad, Richard Foster," I say.

Javen approaches Dad and extends his hand. "Dr. Foster, I'm pleased to see you once again."

"You're Vihann's son, right?" Dad asks.

Javen bows his head slightly. "Yes, sir."

The corners of my lips tip up at his evident respect for my father. Javen is too honest for me to ever think he is simply putting on a show. Dad's gaze flits my way and I try to remain sturdy beneath the questions burning in his eyes.

"I saw you several years ago when my wife and I were first on Arcadia." Dad's face takes on a serious expression, I'm sure with the recollection of those memories. But then he turns his sharp attention back to me and raises an eyebrow. "You haven't told anything about Javen."

A blush snakes its way up my neck. "Sorry. It's complicated and there was—is just way too much to share . . . right now." I have no desire to tell him that the Starfire bonded Javen and me together. Its sounds crazy and I don't even know what to make of the story myself. I continue to meet Dad's searching gaze, hoping my features are schooled into innocence.

Dad flattens his lips into a straight line.

"*Dad*, I'll explain everything later. We need to find Owens's contact, okay?" I re-direct his attention away from my fluttering pulse and reddening face.

"Fine," Dad says and taps on his Connect. "But I'm making it a point to stay alive so I can hear this story."

"Deal." I let out a small, nervous chuckle while rolling my eyes, relieved that he's not pressing for answers. But then I remember there's not much right now to laugh about and my smile fades.

I return my attention to Javen and fill him in on everything that has happened.

"So, you can't use the Starfire?" he asks, concern filling his eyes.

"Not until my body makes the adjustment."

Javen curses under his breath. "I don't know why I hadn't thought of this before now. This sort of sickness can happen to us as children when we learn to control the energy, if we progress too fast. I should have warned you."

"I don't think it would have mattered if you had. I would have tried to save those people anyway."

Javen brushes flyaway strands off my face and tucks them behind my ear. "I know."

His touch sends a thrill through me, even more so when I realize Dad hasn't noticed. I quickly attempt to change the subject before he does. "What about Vihann?"

A muscle in Javen's jaw twitches.

"Still? He won't budge?"

"The earthquakes are picking up on Paxon, too. This means the mining process is still happening."

This time *I* curse under my breath. Not that I believed Hammond would halt production but because we're running out of time. "Are you going to call on your people? Let them decide for themselves?"

Javen straightens. "When it's time, I will."

"I have all the information uploaded," Dad interrupts us. "I don't have a contact name yet, but I have a location and a map to get there."

"Where?" I ask.

"Smack in the middle of Primaro," he says.

Javen studies the map, lines appearing between his dark brows.

I glance around in search of the Rover. By some weird luck, the vehicle is still there, hidden next to a clump of trees across from where Dad's lab used to be.

"Javen can't transport all three of us without draining too much of his Starfire energy. It's too risky. So, we can take the Rover closer to the city and then walk the rest of the way in." I glance at Javen. "Will you be able to cloak both of us in Primaro?"

"Hammond is intermittently using the Starfire Inhibitor to keep Alku away from the city. But I knew you may need to return to Primaro, so I visited the city on foot and was able to cloak my presence. It appears she moved the Inhibitor to the mining area since that site needs her protection most."

"There are less guarded areas in Primaro?" Dad asks.

"Yes, and unless those areas have changed over the last several days, I believe I know where we can go and which places to avoid."

"Okay, let's go." I wave Javen and Dad toward the Rover and then race ahead. My legs are growing much stronger, and I actually feel nearly healed. But there's no way I'm taking a chance on using the Starfire before I'm confident that I can handle the energy exchange.

I make it to the Rover and hop in the front seat. Dad rides shotgun and doesn't even say anything about me driving. But he's the one who taught me how to run manual overrides on a vehicle last year, and I scored one hundred percent on my driving test. Javen hops in the back, directly behind me.

I activate the controls and bring up the coordinates to the city from here. The engine lightly hums as I swipe my hand over the dash, and then the tires spin, moving us forward. I peer over my shoulder quickly at Javen and ask, "First time in a car?"

"New experiences are a good thing," he says.

△ △ △

I bring the Rover to a stop a half-mile from the city and hide the vehicle in the trees as best as I can. I mark the location on my Connect to easily relocate our ride when we return. As of yet, we've seen no ships overhead or scouts out in the forest. But one can never be too careful.

Dad opens the map on his Connect again. "I have a building and a suite number. Owens had access to a series of encrypted messages calling for a meeting in person with his contact. I'm replying now. If we don't hear anything back, best we can hope is that our contact is there when we arrive." Dad taps across the hologram and hits send. A second later the device beeps, and automatically the hologram disengages. "Okay. I told them we'd meet in twenty-five minutes. That's our estimated time of arrival."

We make our way toward the city, and when we're just on the outskirts, Javen takes my hand and clasps onto Dad.

"We have plenty of time," Javen says. "There's no need while we're cloaked to make any sudden moves or try to run. To remain invisible to the humans in Primaro, I need to be touching you at all times."

Both Dad and I agree, and we set off.

Inside the city, it's as if a black cloud hangs over everything. Instead of the beautiful, partially organic but cosmopolitan atmosphere Dad designed for this place, the city feels more like a prison. Guards are dotted among the pedestrians on the street, and at least three times already, I've seen vehicles drive past with the

World Senate logo on the side. Even the citizens' faces seem solemn, and conversations we pass by are in hushed tones.

Dad checks his Connect and indicates for us to take the next right, and as we do, the buildings all start to look familiar. This is the street the Capitol building is on. My heart picks up speed. The last time we were here, Irene and I were captured by Hammond and then jailed.

Luckily, Dad gestures to a building across the way. By the address, we must be seven blocks from the Capitol. I'm not sure if I could handle going back there again. Plus, I'm sure the building is protected from anyone who is using the Starfire nearby. We cross the street inside a glowing cyan cloud. Thankfully, no one has yet noticed our presence.

We wait for a pedestrian to enter for the automatic door to slide open. When someone approaches, we race through as quickly as possible, all while holding onto Javen. I spot the stairwell. I breathe in deeply, and then we begin our climb to the ninth floor. My legs burn as we reach the landing, and I check on Dad, who's winded. For a man his age, he stays in shape, but nine flights is a lot, especially when coupled with the stress of getting here.

"You okay?" I whisper.

"Will be in a minute," he pants.

As we wait, my chest tingles with nervousness. Who knows whether we are walking into a trap? But it's a chance we need to take. "I think I should reveal myself first, and after we assess the safety, you can, Dad."

"No way, Cassi. I'm not putting you into any more danger than necessary. I'm the one doing this. You and Javen hang back. You may not need to reveal yourselves at all."

I close my eyes for a second. I want to argue but instead lean into his ear. I reach for and grip my gun. "I've got your back. Team Foster, okay?"

Dad's lips curve into a sad smile. "Team Foster."

Javen releases Dad, and the cyan glow around him dissipates. Just seeing it disappear from him forces my breathing to increase. Gripping Javen's hand, I follow Dad as he strides directly toward the unit. I check the time, and we are right on schedule. I draw in a deep, fortifying breath as Dad types to the contact.

I'm here.

Dad straightens his back and drops his shoulders while approaching the door. A rustling sound comes from inside and then the door cracks open. A man I haven't seen before peers out.

Javen grips my fingers tighter, and I squeeze the handle of my weapon with my other hand.

The man, who has dark wavy hair and appears of Indian decent, raises his eyebrows when he sees Dad but says nothing. Instead, he opens the door more widely and gestures Dad inside. Dad glances around and doesn't move his feet, and I know he's giving us a brief second to get inside. Javen and I rush through the opening. Then Dad follows the silent instructions.

When the man shuts the door, he crosses his arms over his chest. "Dr. Foster? Aren't you supposed to be dead?" His voice still maintains the slightest hint of an Indian accent.

Dad presses his lips together. "I have heard this rumor."

The man bows his head slightly. "I apologize, but I must scan you for weapons."

"I understand," Dad says.

The man taps on his Connect and extends his wrist toward Dad. The device beeps and then a beam extends from his Connect. The man runs it up and down Dad's body, then indicates for him to turn. Dad obeys, holding his hands in the air. Good thing that I'm the one with the pistol.

"Thank you." The man nods and taps twice on his Connect. "He's clean."

Javen snaps his head toward the front door as if he heard something. Or someone. Before I hear anything, the lock clicks and in walks one of the last people I had expected to see.

Luca Powell.

My heart leaps into my throat. Was Matt Owens a double agent? A traitor, too?

I flit my attention to Dad as his face turns ashen. He knows what I told him about Luca and his traitorous behavior. He also saw him on the spy video from General Atkins. Dad has no idea where I am in the room, but he holds his hand up slightly as if to tell me to hold my ground, but not enough to alert them that Javen and I are here. I squeeze Javen's hand so tightly I think I might hurt him, but he does nothing to stop me.

Another person follows behind Luca. Alina. She peers around the room and back out into the hall, then closes the door behind her. She walks to the other man and stands beside him. Anger burns in my core against her. This girl has tricked me too many times. Why does she have to be here now? Part of me wants to shoot the lot of them and be done with this sordid business. But I know I could never do so in cold blood.

My eyes waver among all the people in the room. No one is speaking and it's driving me crazy.

"Dr. Foster," Luca says and walks toward Dad with his hand extended. Dad doesn't take it and Luca drops his hand to his side. "We had no idea you were alive."

Dad narrows his eyes. "You know I'm unarmed. If you're going to kill me, I would rather skip the formalities."

Luca tips his head and his eyes widen in surprise. "I'm not going to kill you. I'm simply surprised you're here. When we received Owens's encrypted message to meet, we weren't quite sure what to do as we'd gotten word he was killed in the city bombing the other day. That's why I sent Madan in here first." He looks to the other man.

I look back to Javen, but he seems no less confused by this than me.

"Are you needing asylum?" Luca asks. "It will be difficult, but I believe we can get you off Arcadia eventually, if need be."

"Asylum?" Dad asks. "What are you talking about?"

My mind spins with all I know about Luca, and I can't stand waiting anymore. I release from Javen, and the blue-green glow around us vanishes. "What are you talking about, Luca?" I growl and point my weapon at him.

"Cassi!" Dad scolds.

Luca takes a step backward and throws his hands up chest-high. Alina and Madan inch away in surprise. Luca stares at me and then to Javen, whose right hand now glows cyan.

"Whoa," Luca says to me. "This obviously is *not* what you think it is."

"Then what is it?" I snarl. "I saw you, Luca. I saw you more than once. You are a snake." I whip my attention to Alina. "And you . . . you are no better."

"You only think you know what I am, Cassi," Luca says. "And you have me all wrong."

"Then how are you still alive when Hirata and Cooper are dead?" I glare at him, clenching my pistol.

Luca grits his teeth together.

"Because he was ordered to plead, if he had the opportunity," Alina says. "Luca is one of the only insiders left who Hammond trusts."

I look at her. "Who ordered him?"

"That's not something we can reveal," she says. "But you'll need to trust us."

"I'm not trusting either of you," I say.

"There aren't a lot of options in this situation, Cassi," Luca says. "Hammond is calling in more battleships from Earth. The fleet is moving through the Space Fold now. My people want to get anyone of high rank to safety, and there's not much time."

"Listen," Alina says. "I get your lack of trust. But if Dr. Foster is alive, we need to at least get him out of Primaro." She holds an object my way, and it's not a weapon.

It's my mom's journal.

Chapter 22

Fuming, I march up to Alina, pistol still in hand, and snatch the leather-bound journal from her grasp.

"If you're giving this back to me, why would you steal it in the first place?"

Shame blankets Alina's face. Her demeanor is entirely different than the girl I knew at the dorm. That girl seemed immature, careless, and self-absorbed. "It was a spur-of-the-moment type of thing," she says. "Our people were looking for solutions in using the Starfire to help us. I saw the journal and had a hunch it might be Dr. Foster's, and that it might contain data we could use. But when I discovered what it really was, I felt terrible. I didn't mean to take something belonging to your mother. I've carried her journal with me ever since I took it, so her words never fell into the wrong hands. I didn't even tell anyone but Luca that I had it."

"How did you know it's hers? Did you read it?" I snap.

So much has been stolen from me.

Javen touches my shoulder and I glance at him. The glow around his hand is gone, but fire still burns in his eyes.

"I could never get the lock open," Alina interrupts and I turn my attention back to her. "But I was able to see the name under the strap."

I pry my finger under the piece of leather and see the tiny inscription of my mom's name.

Isabel Foster

"I shouldn't have taken it. But we have been grasping at straws for data." The emotion in her eyes makes me want to believe Alina. But this entire situation is completely unbelievable.

"So, you want *me* to tell you what's inside?" I snap.

She arches a brow. "If the information is useful to our cause."

Dad steps toward Luca and the others. "Thank you for returning the journal, but can one of you please explain who you really are and what is going on?"

"There's not a lot of time," Alina says. "But essentially, I was sent to Arcadia by the group I work for to keep tabs on certain people. Meeting Cassi in the dorm was only a happy accident. But living next to her changed my mission entirely."

"What are you talking about, Alina? You're like sixteen . . . maybe seventeen," I sneer. "Is Alina really your name?"

She shrugs. "I know it's difficult to believe, and this is the last setting I wanted to be in to convince you. But I only look young. My appearance is part of my cover."

"And you?" Dad says to Luca. "What are you? Forty? And do you work for these people, too?"

Luca smirks. "No, I'm definitely not forty. After Hammond told me what she was doing and how the plan would affect this planet and the Alku, I knew I couldn't follow her. But I needed to bide my time and play along. I hoped being on the Board would help me influence the way situations played out. I'll admit that I was weak, though. Then Alina became my assistant and Hirata came into power. Afterward, Alina approached me in secret to feel out my intentions. When Hammond returned and made the arrests, we planned for me to make a plea. It was a longshot, but I was able to convince Hammond I was only there to spy for her. She bought my lie."

"We have to go, sir," Madan says and glances at his Connect. "You've already been away from the Capitol building for too long."

"Honestly, there isn't that much we can do at this point, though. If the Alku are still refusing to attack . . ." He eyes Javen. "And getting any rebel ships through the Turner Space Fold is proving impossible. It's too heavily guarded. The living members of the World Senate who side with us would help, if they could, but it's too dangerous to reveal their positions. The best we can offer you right now is to keep you alive, Dr. Foster. We can rebuild confidence and attempt again later."

"The Alku may be willing to defend themselves," Javen says.

"We have a plan to reclaim one of the mining sites and take out the device blocking the Starfire energy," I add. "But we were really hoping Owens's contact—you—might be able to secure the help of the World Senate members who are still sympathetic to the cause."

"For that," Alina says, "our hands are tied. If there were a way to get ships to Arcadia without using the TSF, I'm certain the option would be considered by the underground Senate members. But right now, their help is impossible."

I always knew getting outside help was a longshot. But knowing we're on our own sets a pit in my stomach.

"Well," Dad says. "We didn't come here to go into hiding. And if you're just going to sit by and let this travesty happen, then we need to leave." He looks to Javen. "You can get us back out of the city, right?"

"Yes, sir," Javen says.

Still not really sure if we're safe, I holster my pistol in my waistband. If Luca wanted to kill us or take us into custody, he would have done so already. But he could always just be afraid of what Javen might do. I grip onto the journal and turn my attention to Dad. "Let's leave. We have to get back and prepare."

"Get back where? For what?" Alina asks.

I look at her. There's no way I'm telling any of them about the Intersection.

"There's a war going on, Alina," I say. "If you haven't noticed. We need to prepare the troops we have."

"You won't win," Luca warns as he walks to the door and opens it.

"Sometimes you still have to try," Javen says and then grabs my hand and pulls me to Dad. A cyan glow illuminates us as he clasps Dad's upper arm. Javen nods to me, and we rush out the door.

I almost expect Luca and Alina to have a small portable device able to block the Starfire energy so guards can jump out in surprise to arrest us. But nothing happens.

Outside, we hurry toward the city's edge. Javen navigates us back down the safest streets where his Starfire energy can still be maintained. As we near the perimeter of the city, my and Dad's Connects buzz and a holographic message appears above the screen, rotating and flashing in red.

Emergency Alert

This is probably where I find out Luca and Alina were lying the entire time. "Slow down," I say to Javen. "We should see whatever this is." I look out toward the forest. We are so close to being outside of Primaro. My muscles tense with anxiety.

> *Citizens of Primaro. This is an emergency alert. Please return to your homes. If this is not possible, make your way to the lower levels of the nearest building.*

The message repeats itself but gives no further details. An alarm blares from behind us, signaling emergency procedures in the city. Everyone was trained on these before we arrived on Arcadia. But I'm not sure anyone thought we might actually have to use them for a reason like war.

We pick up the pace again, but Javen suddenly slows us and stops. His eyes swirl with cyan, and then he closes them and inhales deeply. When he opens them again, I know by the tension on his face that whatever just happened isn't positive.

"Wirrin is summoning me. The army used the portal and are already on this side. The troops are in a holding pattern but are waiting to attack."

Dad's expression falls. "Why didn't they wait?"

"He's not sharing his reasons. All I know is that he wants us outside of the mining site."

"Before we left, they were willing to wait." Dad's eyebrows knit in confusion. "Why would Wirrin try and fight again?"

"But the army hasn't attacked yet, right?" I confirm.

"Not from what I could tell in the summons. But he is agitated," Javen says. "I suggest getting to him immediately."

It's still a half-mile to the Rover, and the mine is on the opposite side of Primaro from our location now. "Can you transport the three of us without draining your energy too much?"

Dad reaches into his pocket and pulls out my Starfire from the Intersection. My chest tenses at the sight. Analya said I would know when I was ready to use the Starfire again, and something inside of me tells me I'm not.

"I know the Alku can't normally refresh their connection to the Starfire unless they're on the Paxon side. Javen told me," I say.

"In the time that you were healing," Dad says, "Wirrin and the other Alku discovered that the

Intersection crystals allow the recharging to happen anywhere."

"So, have they been renewing their connection with the Intersection Starfire?" I ask. Panic works its way through my chest and arms. "All of them?"

"As the Starfire was being harvested for energy, it took over and refueled them. The process was automatic."

"Why didn't you tell me?" I ask.

Dad studies me for a second. "This is a good thing."

"Maybe, but I'm still not sure. When I first found you in the Intersection you . . . you were affected."

"What do you mean?" Dad's face scrunches into an almost offended expression.

"You don't remember?" I ask.

"I admit, I *did* feel different when I first began studying the Starfire there. But I figured that experience was typical. My body adjusted, and everything is normal now. It's the same as when your body adjusted."

"You might be right, Dad." I look to his hand still clutching the crystal. "But Wirrin told me a story about how the Intersection Starfire can be all-consuming for the Alku." I move my attention to Javen. "Did you sense any of this from your uncle just now?"

He thinks for a moment. "Possibly, but it may only be his desire to save Paxon." Javen says. "I'm going to take the risk and take us to Wirrin."

I open my mouth to protest, but before I can, the force of transporting hits my body as Javen squeezes my hand. I gasp when we jolt to our new location. Javen releases Dad and me, and then Dad shoves the Intersection Starfire into Javen's hand.

Javen's eyes go wide, and he inhales deeply, then relaxes. He turns to me, eyes swirling a brighter blue-green than I've ever seen. Within seconds, his eyes return to brown. "You weren't kidding when you said this was powerful." He hands the crystal back to Dad. "Before we go, I need to initiate the summoning to the Alku still on Paxon."

Dad and I say nothing, and so Javen falls into a trance-like state, closing his eyes.

After a moment he opens his eyes and points ahead of us. "The camp should be this way."

"Will they come?" I ask.

"Many of my people are frightened about what is happening on our side. But I believe so."

I press down my fears. Now Javen has used the Intersection Starfire. But my greater concern is for all the Alku who entered the Intersection and used the Starfire there, as well.

The three of us sprint in the direction Javen indicated, and after a few minutes, we reach the hidden camp among the trees. I search the faces of both the Alku and the humans. Several of the Alku bow their heads to

Javen. We finally find Wirrin in the crowd. He extends his hand to Javen, though his serious expression remains.

"Why are you here already?" Javen demands, ignoring Wirrin's hand. "You were asked to wait."

Wirrin's lips form a thin line. "The people were becoming restless."

"*You* are leading them, Wirrin," Dad says. "And we had an agreement."

Analya comes up from behind. "We used the portal device on the other side and sent a few people through. We were able to get word to General Atkins's spy. It was either act now or have no chance." She hands the device back to Dad.

I look around and can't find my friends. "Where are Beda and Max? And Irene?"

"They are part of the team who volunteered to infiltrate the mining facility," Wirrin says. "The three are already on their way."

"What?" I demand. "My friends are going to get killed!"

"Someone has to disable the Inhibitor for us to move in," Analya says. "Irene has the skills to do what needs to be done, and Max and Beda are protecting her to ensure she gets inside. Once the device is disabled, Beda will summon us."

My friends are putting themselves into so much danger and I'm not able to help them. My body stiffens and I fidget with my Connect, wanting to contact Max or Irene, but I'm too late.

"And the modified refugee ships?" Dad looks around, but they're not here. Not that we would be able to see them from our hidden position anyway.

"The portal is ready when we need the ships to come," Wirrin says. "You can use your device and open the portal for them. The ships should be able to exit directly over the mining site."

My mind returns to the Emergency Alert in Primaro. "But if the army hasn't attacked yet," I ask Dad and Javen, "then why the alarms? Why have everyone return to their homes?"

"That would be our diversion," Wirrin says. "General Atkins had false intel sent to Hammond, alerting her that the three missing refugee ships were sighted and then re-cloaked. This is, of course, untrue. However, our story sounds plausible enough after the way you evacuated them to the Intersection. If Hammond believes the ships will attack the city, then her focus may not be on the mine."

Analya goes into a brief trance. "Beda's team has disabled the Starfire Inhibitor. We must move now."

Wirrin straightens, and his hand glows blue-green. All the Alku turn his way, including Javen. Their hands illuminate as well, as if a cyan fire were lit in the forest. Wirrin waves them forward. To war. And this time I can't save them.

Chapter 23

Javen turns to me while I watch the Alku charge. Then, to my surprise, at least a hundred more Alku appear around us, the ones who have decided to follow Javen. Pride fills me with his willingness to be the leader he was born to be. Javen yells for them to follow Wirrin, and without question, the army obeys. Behind us, the crackle and roar of a giant portal sounds. Javen's face lights up cyan from the glow and his eyes gleam.

Javen clutches my arm, and I flinch from the energy radiating from his Starfire energy. "I don't know if this is the beginning or the end." Without another word, his mouth collides with mine. Fire curls through my veins as his breath becomes mine. I nearly drop my mom's journal but somehow hold it tight in one hand. His touch unravels me until the world spins away for a few heartbeats of time. Here, only Javen and I exist. I return his kiss with more fervor than I have ever expressed before. This need, this fear, his presence—it's everything. So much so, that when he finally pulls away, the sense of loss is devastating.

"Javen, *you* are my beginning and end." I can barely get the words out. A sob knots in my throat and tears prick the back of my eyes. He folds me into his strong arms and holds me tight to his chest as if he'll never let go. Then he does, and I heave in a ragged breath as he races to join the rest of his people. He can't leave them to fight on their own.

"That boy is in love with you," Dad says softly from behind. "I've seen the look before."

I twist around to him, and he holds the Starfire out to me. Any embarrassment I might have had for sharing such an intense, intimate kiss with Javen in front of Dad is gone. In the next hour, many of us will likely die. And right now, Dad is trying to give me the Starfire.

I glance at the crystal and back to his face. "I'm not sure if I should take it. I might not be ready."

"Something tells me you are."

Gingerly, I pluck the gem from his palm and suppress the urge to welcome a flood of the crystal's energy into my body. Barely looking at the Starfire, I grab the necklace and pull the chain over my head.

Dad's eyes well up with tears and I fall into his arms. "This wasn't what Arcadia was supposed to be like,

Daddy," I cry into his neck. A blast sounds from behind and I flinch. "How can one planet's salvation be the another's doom? It's not fair."

Dad pulls back from me and then places his hands on my shoulders. He doesn't answer my question. Instead, he gently squeezes my upper arms before his hands fall back to his sides.

He steps away from me, but I grab his hand. "How do you know Javen loves me?"

Dad's lips quirk into a sad smile. "Because the look in his eyes is the same one I gave your mom every morning when I was privileged enough to share my life with hers."

The words make my breath hitch.

"I want to send you far from here, Cassi. But nowhere is safe. Not Earth, not Primaro, and you can't hide in the Intersection forever. You've made a connection to this planet and its people I don't entirely understand. All I know is that you are a key to setting things right again."

I gape at him, not wholly believing his words but also knowing them to be the truth.

"Are you coming?" he asks.

I want to say yes, but apparently my feet refuse to move. "I need a moment."

Dad nods. "I love you, Cassi."

"I love you too, Daddy."

He exhales a quick breath and then sprints toward a group of armed refugees who haven't joined the fight yet. He taps on the portal device and I whip around just in time for the two modified refugee ships to appear overhead and take off toward the mining site.

Alone and the last to leave the area, I collapse in a heap on the forest floor. I wipe away the river of tears spilling down my cheeks.

My mom's journal rests solidly in my hands. I turn the small book over and study the plain leather. I trace along the lock, my brows furrowed. Then, as if compelled, I take my necklace off and hold the crystal to the locked front.

The gem pulses and illuminates. I hold my breath, waiting. Hoping. And then it happens. The lock clicks open. My breath hitches.

An explosion rumbles from behind me. I snap my gaze toward it, but I don't see anything. So, I push up to my feet and scan the area.

"I don't have time to deal with this." I bury the journal under fern-like foliage growing beneath a tree. Then I tap my Connect and mark this spot so I can make it back if—*when*—this is over. I throw a few more handfuls of underbrush on top of the book for good measure and then race to the overlook. Once there, I feel for my pistol; it's there. But it's not the best solution, anyway. I've never fired one of those things and would probably be dead in a flash if I tried. I fumble for my Starfire, my only hope.

I hold the crystal in my hand and curl my fingers around it. But I'm just not able to focus, so instead I look below the ridge and watch the chaos. The Starfire Inhibitor has been either destroyed or stopped. Dotted bursts of light illuminate the site sporadically. But to hold back the Alku, soldier bots have been released to protect the mine. From the south, Hammond's ships approach. Shots are fired from one of the upgraded refugee hovers. Despite the Starfire power source upgrades, I'm not sure if our two upgraded escape ships will be powerful enough to control Hammond's ten other ships.

The refugee ships shoot bolts of cyan lasers at the enemy, but Hammond's vessels return the fire in full force. On the ground, several refugees and Alku are already down.

Fear gallops through my body and sends ice shards up my spine. I have no idea what to do or whether there's anything I can do with the Starfire to help. Just stopping the battle won't solve the problem. If Hammond's forces are not destroyed, this will continue. And I can't hide the Alku forever in the Intersection. It's not meant for them to live there anyway. I'm sure of that.

Another explosion rips from below and jolts me from my thoughts. I clench the Starfire and let my body open as a vessel. If I die, then I die. But I can't stand by and let all these people kill each other if nothing can be solved by their sacrifices. And if this battle gets out of control, the mine may be damaged further, making it impossible to stop Paxon's destruction. I need to transport the Alku out of here since the bots have probably already transmitted the feed. Just when I think my pounding heart can't handle another rush of panic, the crystal's warm energy fills me, and any fear remaining falls through my fingers as I let myself go.

A blast of light erupts from me, and I grit my teeth against the caustic sensation of being ripped into a galaxy of a billion stars. Pain travels my entire body and my mind reels. This could be the end—of me, of the Alku, Paxon, Arcadia, perhaps even Earth. My jaw aches as I clench it even harder, a relieved whimper escaping my chapped lips when the pain finally subsides. I draw in a much-needed breath. My chest and limbs tingle as if blood has pushed through my once-constricted veins. My mind swirls in a cyan haze.

With a loud crack, the world comes back to me full force and my thoughts buzz with the Alku. It's as if I'm not only summoning them but also hearing their thoughts and intentions. Through the buzz of communication, I make out Wirrin and Javen issuing battle instructions to the fighting Alku. Responses come through, and I struggle to make sense of their replies. I drop to my knees and throw my hands to my ears, but of course, the voices persist because the sound is in my head. And what I hear gives me pause. All the voices have turned from a position of defense to one of overthrowing. Something has changed. Using the Starfire from the Intersection has shifted the Alku's thoughts.

This can't be happening.

I reach out to summon Javen, but nothing returns. It's as if he's blocking any contact from me. I close my eyes and focus on quieting the noise. Wary, I look down to the still-churning chaos, and a shadow passes across the ground below. Several gigantic battle cruisers glide through the sky. Cruisers that were not there before. Hammond's new incoming forces must be coming through the TSF, close to the planet's atmosphere.

If the Alku's goal has changed, what are the consequences for the humans fighting with them? Are they enemies now, too? I peer around the ridge and suck in a sharp breath. Where is everyone? Did everyone already join the fight below, including Dad? I tap my Connect and use the voice function.

"Dad," I say. Nothing comes back through, so I change gears.

"Irene," I say. "Are you there?" No reply.

I try again.

"Cassi." Irene's shaky voice finally comes through. "Where are you?"

"I'm still on the ridge. What's going on down there?" My breath picks up as I speak.

The hologram function activates, and I can see Irene with Max behind her. "We're pinned down near the mine entrance. After we took out the Inhibitor, Beda got this weird look in her eyes and abandoned us. Then everything went nuts."

Behind Irene and Max, a blast of cyan light illuminates the mine's walls. Max fires a few laser shots in return.

"Are the Alku attacking you?" I yell.

"I think the army turned on anyone from Earth."

My chest tenses at the confirmation. But there is no way Javen would do this. I know him.

I look at the mine entrance. I have to get down there.

A war cruiser lands and an army of soldiers pours out of the ship within seconds. I feel the sudden, furious urge to destroy the vessel with my Starfire energy. But I resist falling into the Alku's now-aggressive energy. Stopping them is one thing; wiping them out is another.

"I'm coming to you," I say to Irene and then click off the Connect without waiting for her reply. If I leave them, they will die, and for nothing. When I get there, I'll figure out where Dad is.

I focus on the entrance of the mine and visualize myself there. When my eyes open, I quickly duck behind a wall and activate my Connect again. "Send me your exact coordinates," I say to Irene.

The directions come through, and I display them on the map. Max and Irene are around a nearby bend. I close my eyes and reappear next to Max. My heart fills with joy to see them both still alive. But it's quickly suppressed when a ball of light explodes in front of us. The sound of laser weapons echoes up above. Hammond's army must be closing in.

"I need to summon Javen," I say. "We must work together, or this will fail. I never should have brought the Alku into the Intersection. I knew that place was dangerous for them. Their access was blocked for a reason to ensure Javen's race didn't use the dimension's Starfire." I look to Max and Irene. "But first, I should get you to safety. And the Intersection is my only option right now."

"Cassi," Irene says. "There's no time. It's a bloodbath out there. If there's a way to stop the battle now, we should do that instead."

I look to Max, and he agrees. "Do it. We've got your back."

I squeeze the Starfire in my palm and focus on its energy, then push it outward to stop the madness. A cyan burst starts at my core and reverberates out like a giant wave of energy. I have no idea what is going to happen. All I want is to stop the killing.

With a zap, I come to, and all around me is a cyan glow. The world seems to be in ultra-slow motion or underwater. Except for me. Max and Irene are nearly frozen except for micro movements. I reach for Irene and tap her on the shoulder. I inhale deeply and unlock her from her transfixed state. When I do, she breaks from the trance and her breath comes in erratic pants. She looks around as I do the same to Max.

"What's going on?" Max asks.

"I don't know yet," I say, but the only sound I can hear around us is the slight buzzing of Starfire energy. With caution, I emerge from our hiding place. Outside and as far as I can see, everything looks the same. Nearly frozen. A cyan blast from an angry Alku's hand is suspended in mid-air. Hammond's soldiers stand with weapons pointed high. One of the gigantic ships is frozen in the air, mid-explosion.

"I have to find Javen," I say. "He can help me stop this battle."

I scan the area but don't see him.

"There," Max says and points to my left.

I follow his finger and see Javen in the distance, and I pause. A blood-curdling shiver moves down my body. The anger on his face shoots pain into my stomach and I want to retch. But I suppress the nauseating urge and race for him instead, the others following behind.

Fear writhes its way through my insides as we get closer. But I keep my attention focused only on him.

"Cassi!" Irene yells from behind.

I skid to a stop to see what she wants. Next to her is Dad, frozen and clutching the portal device in one hand and a weapon in the other. I run to him and place my hand on his shoulder. He blinks twice and stumbles back a step.

"What the . . ." he says.

"Dad."

He looks around, then flits his attention to me. "What's going on, Cassi?"

"I used my Starfire to stop the battle. The Starfire from the Intersection has altered the Alku, and I need to fix my mistake."

Dad glances around, and the wide-mouthed, shocked look on his face wears the memory of everything horrible now flooding back to him—the calculation error we both made. I knew the Intersection Starfire changed people, and now he does, too. But I don't have time to explain the experience to him. I have no idea how long this frozen state will last. I can already feel the weight of the Starfire's energy slipping through my grasp.

I finally reach Javen and draw my brows together. His eyes swirl with anger instead of the gentleness I know.

With shaking fingers, I touch his hand, and in an instant, he unfreezes and grips my fingers.

I hold my breath as he bares his teeth at me.

"Javen," I cry out. "It's me, Cassi!"

He lets out a low growl as if he doesn't know me.

"Javen, please. Fight this . . . this anger. It's not you."

With a shove, Javen releases my hand and pushes me away from him.

"Cassi," Dad says close by. "You need to back away."

I do as he says, but my legs will only move so quickly. I stare at Javen's hand, which now glows cyan.

"You humans are stealing everything from us. And we will take our planet back!" he roars at me.

I think of my hidden laser pistol. But I can pretty much guarantee that I'll never get it out in time. I can't shoot Javen anyway. Unsure of what to do, I choose my words carefully. "We need to fix this together. It's the only chance for peace." I close my eyes and clear my mind in attempt to summon him, connect to his mind. But a force shoves my thoughts back and I flick my eyes back open to the horrible scene.

"No," he growls, and with that single word, our bond disintegrates. I shudder in a breath from the pain of the unexpected severance, as if my insides are being ripped out. The anger hardens his beautiful features and the pain in my gut intensifies. Doesn't he feel the loss? Is the grief shredding through his body, like it is in mine? He gives away nothing, if so, and instead puts his palms up into the air. A bolt of cyan energy shoots from his hands into the sky and the frozen battlefield thaws within a wild beat of my heart.

The scene roars to life. Javen's hands fly forward, and another bolt shoots for me. I seize up, muscles tight, waiting for the hit. And then I'm falling, forced to the ground and out of the way. The bolt hits Dad square in the shoulder, and he buckles and tumbles to the ground beside me.

Chapter 24

grab for Dad's limp body and scream for Max and Irene. Both turn my way as they shoot their laser guns at the Alku now charging for them from behind Javen. They get to my side and Irene attempts to pull me to my feet, but instead, I yank her down and grab Max by the leg. Mustering all the energy inside of me, I visualize us inside the Intersection and rip the four of us through.

On the other side, I glance down under the starlight at Dad and his barely breathing chest.

"We can't let him die!" I screech.

My mind reels as images of Javen blasting Dad replay over and over again in my mind. Seeing him changed guts me. Everything I had on this planet . . . *everything* has been stolen from me.

I begin to heave with unreleased grief but force myself back to reality, to the present. Max is by my side and no one else. Panic resets in my bloodstream and I rush out, "Where's Irene and the rest of the people who stayed behind?"

"She ran to the lab. There are some basic medical supplies back there. The other people might be at camp." Terror washes over his face and then he whispers, "Do you think the Alku are coming after us?"

Dad's portal device still juts out from his pocket. I retrieve the black device and hand it to Max. "I'm pretty sure this was the only one, and from what I can tell, the Alku can't cross into the Intersection without it or me. But since the Alku have now absorbed the Intersection Starfire, I have no idea if they'll eventually be able to."

It's not a satisfying answer and the tension still shows on Max's face. Avoiding him, I return my attention back to Dad. What if the Starfire can heal him? I pull the crystal from my neck and place the gem to his chest. The second I do, his body tenses.

"What are you doing, Cassi?" Max yells. "You saw what the Starfire just did. Who knows what will happen if he wakes up?"

Everything in me wants to listen to him and remove the crystal, but a voice in my mind tells me to leave the Intersection's gem where it is, to funnel myself with energy.

If you need to take me, I tell the Starfire, *do it. Just don't take Dad. He needs to live.* Warmth fills my core and spreads up my chest and into my neck and arms. Memories of my life swirl through my mind, both good and bad . . . life with my parents, growing up, the memories of Javen's life mixed with mine. Like a whirlwind, I integrate the Starfire's power with who I am—an imperfect person who wants nothing more than all these wrongs set right again.

"Please work," I whisper. "I just want my Dad back right now."

I open my eyes and find my body slumped over Dad's.

Rolling up to sit, my eyes focus on him, and then I see his breathing has returned to normal. His eyelids flutter open.

"Daddy!" I cry out, throwing my arms around his neck.

He groans, and I jerk back.

"Am I hurting you?"

"A little bit." He sits up and looks around, confusion pinching his brows and mouth. "What happened?"

"Can you stand?" I ask while searching for Irene and Max, who are now standing a good distance away with wide-eyed looks on their faces.

"Please help," I call out. They look at each other and then jog my way.

Max steps in, reaches toward Dad and takes his hand. "Do you think you can stand?"

Dad nods and blinks several times, as if he's trying to wake up. He takes Max's hand, and Max tugs up, pulling him to his feet.

"Lean on me if you need to," Max says.

Dad shifts, a bit dizzy on his feet, and then straightens. "Thank you," he mutters before Max leads him toward the lab.

Irene stares down at me for several seconds and then finally offers her hand to help me up.

"Why are you looking at me like that?" I ask, wavering my attention between her and Dad to ensure Dad stays upright.

"Cassi," she says, "when you used the Starfire on your Dad, something happened."

"What?" I ask, placing the necklace back around my neck.

"I don't quite know what I was seeing, but everything around us was glowing . . . on fire almost."

"Fire?"

"Yeah. I've seen some pretty amazing things in the last few days, but what just happened tops that off." She grabs my arm and pulls me toward the lab. Dad and Max are nearly at the front entrance. "Do you really think we are safe?"

I look around, unsure if I can answer her question truthfully. The Starfire from here changed the Alku, and I and have no idea if just being in such proximity to the fields will negatively change humans, too. Maybe the change just takes longer. "If someone were able to follow us, they would be here by now."

Irene nods, having little choice but to accept the answer.

Inside the lab, my mind is in a complete haze. Still, I check on Dad, who's now resting. Max scanned his vitals before Irene and I even got inside, and he seems to have stabilized.

The walls feel as though they are compressing my body, and all I want to do is go back outside. "I need to be alone for a while," I tell Max and Irene. "I'm taking a walk."

"You really need to rest, and I'm going to find some food around here," Irene says. "And then we need to tell the survivors left behind here what happened. Prepare them for the worst."

"I'd be able to rest better if I had a few minutes to think," I say, the building pressure of my emotions weighing on my chest.

Max looks at Irene. "Let her go."

Irene nods, and I smile at Max. He looks away.

But I don't have the energy to delve into what either of them is going through right now. I will eventually, but I have my own losses to sort through. In a haze, I make my way toward the exit. The Intersection's blue-green cast permeates everything around me. I peer up at the two moons and the cyan gases painting the now night sky.

I reach into my pocket and feel for the Starfire, but it's gone. Confused, I check my other pocket and rush back to the spot where I healed Dad. Something metallic glints from the ground and I rush for it. I retrieve the necklace and search for the crystal pendant, but it's gone.

With a sigh I place the chain around my neck, then scan around the nearly abandoned organic housing constructed by the Alku and refugees. There are a few dull lights, and I see one person wandering in the dark. They don't know anything that happened, and I don't want them to see me right now, so I hurry into a shadow. Beyond them is the hill illuminated by the Starfire field's soft glow from behind the crest.

I avoid the camp, and on the way over to the hill, my body grows heavy. Each step takes effort. Javen severed our bond. He wanted to hurt me, to kill me. The loss sits on my chest until it even hurts to breathe. Is the hope for a connection between humans and Alku now lost? Either the races will destroy each other, or one side will win. But neither really will.

I drop to my knees as the pain building in my heart mounts. What can I do? Any thought that I can fix this situation is ridiculous. Still, I can't help but wonder if there really is anything I can do, something I haven't thought of yet. I sit back on my feet and lay my hands on my lap, palms up.

Mom, if you were here, would you know the answer? Tears stream from my eyes and drop down into my open palms. I squeeze my eyelids shut.

"Why did you have to die?" I yell into the air and out over the Starfire field. "I need your help."

Just as I finish the words, a pulse of light from the field vibrates through my body and I open my eyes to find Mom's journal in my hands.

I hid this on Arcadia and didn't have time to find it again. But since Dad was able to use the Starfire to send the apples to Paxon, maybe I can use the same principle to bring items here. Staring at the cover, I grasp the journal with one hand and touch the lock with the other.

With a click, the lock pops open. My hand glows with a bright cyan hue, and I gasp. How did I do that?

My chest tenses as I stare at the first page, illuminated by the light of the moons and the Starfire field below. My mom's feminine handwriting scrolls over the paper. Dad was right. She started journaling about a year before she died. My heart races, and I quickly flip through the pages to see where the writing ends. I stop at the last entry.

That day. A Tuesday.

The tears begin rolling again, and one drops to the open page and splashes over the paper. I wipe it and a tiny bit of the ink smears. Quickly I center myself and brush the other tears off my face, then glance down at the words with my heart rushing in my ears.

Cassi,

Today is the day. I've played the events out in my head a million times and tried to compose a way for them to turn out differently. But they never do. The visions always end the same way . . . with me gone.

I strain to hold back the tears.

It pains me that I will not be able to join you and Dad on Arcadia. Ever since I "discovered" the planet's atmosphere compatibility nine years ago, I've dreamed of the day our family would set foot there. But I have a secret. I've known about Arcadia since I was a little girl, in my dreams at least.

The visions started when I was five, and the planet came to me every night. Calling me. For some reason, I kept the dreams a secret. But just before your grandfather died the year before you were born, he asked me a strange question. He asked me if the cyan planet had come to me yet. I was confused but ecstatic that someone else might know of it too. Then he showed me the most beautiful cyan crystal and told me a crazy-sounding story.

He told me that he came from another place and that he was the guardian of peace there. But one day, he was so tired of being alone that he used the crystals to help him escape. To release him from his servitude. He was able to open a portal for himself to leave and knew he'd never be able to return. It was a one-way journey for him. He stepped through and found himself not back among his people but here, on Earth. He worked to blend in and hide his identity, and eventually, he married a beautiful redhead. Then they had me. When he died, the crystal was gone. I watched the gem vanish before my eyes.

It all sounded so crazy, the babbles of a man on his deathbed. But I knew all he shared was true. Every word. So, after that, I did everything in my power to find the planet. And when I did, I knew. I convinced your dad to take me there, and we arranged for the journey to happen, and I led your father to the Alku without him knowing how. But on Arcadia, I sensed them, and somehow, the people must have felt I was safe and showed themselves. When they did, I knew this was our home. A new home for Earth.

Mom knew . . . she knew the whole time.

But then the visions changed, and it became clear to me you were the person who needed to come to Arcadia. The planet was calling for you, but for some reason I would not be coming. As much as this knowledge pained me, I worked to make a new life on Arcadia happen, to do what I knew was right.

I don't know how this connection will come about, but you are the key. You'll find a way to bring Arcadia and Paxon back into harmony, as well as bring healing to Earth.

My purpose to get you to Arcadia will be fulfilled, so I can't change my destiny, no matter how much I want to.

Team Foster forever. And tell your dad I love him.

Love always,
Mom

With eyes full and brimming with moisture, I lower the journal. My grandfather is Alku, the One Pure Soul. My mom was Alku.

I am Alku.

Book two of Cassie's journey is at an end, but you can read what happened next in _Parallax_.

△ △ △

Dear Book Lover,

Thank you SO much for your support. I am truly humbled. I would be incredibly grateful if you took the time to **leave a review on Amazon**. Short or long is JUST fine. Your review will make a big difference and help new readers discover The Configured Trilogy.

I would also love it if you joined my book club at **JenettaPenner.com**. When you do, you will receive a FREE printable Configured YA coloring book, as well as YA book news and information on upcoming releases. You can also follow me on **Facebook**.

XXOO,
Jenetta Penner

Other Books by Jenetta Penner

The Configured Trilogy

Configured
Immersed
Actualized

40085038R00166

Made in the USA
San Bernardino, CA
23 June 2019